THE WALL

Also by Elizabeth Lutzeier
The Coldest Winter

THE WALL

Elizabeth Lutzeier

Holiday House / New York

Library of Congress Cataloging-in-Publication Data
Lutzeier, Elizabeth.
The wall / Elizabeth Lutzeier.
p. cm.
Summary: After her mother is killed while trying to escape across
the Berlin Wall in April 1989, Hannah and her father become caught
up in the movement to change the repressive regime in East Germany.
ISBN 0-8234-0987-2
1. Berlin Wall, Berlin, Germany, 1961-1989—Juvenile fiction.
[1. Berlin Wall, Berlin, Germany, 1961-1989—Fiction.   2. Berlin
(Germany)—Fiction.   3. Fathers and daughters—Fiction.]   I. Title.
PZ7.L979554Wal   1992   92-52712   CIP   AC
[Fic]—dc20

For my two favourite Berliners,
Heidi and Thomas Lutzeier

1

HANNAH
Berlin, April 1989

After they shot Hannah's mother, they made her go with her father to a dark building behind the police station. She didn't want to go. But a policewoman came to their flat to collect them and said, 'You only have to take one look at the body. Then you just tell them if you recognize the dead person. That's all.'

The policewoman took Hannah into a large, cold room with high, white walls, where a man was sitting behind a metal desk. Then she went away. After Hannah had stood in front of him and counted to a hundred, the man looked up. 'Take your time,' he said. He had a fat, white, wrinkled face that reminded her of a bulldog.

'Take a good, long look. When you're ready, you can tell us whether you know the woman. Over there. On the bench.' He jerked his head in the direction of a long, thin table on wheels.

'Take a good, long look.'

Papa had said that too, just before they left their flat near the centre of Berlin. 'We'll never see her again. So stay with her as long as you can. And take a good, long look.'

Hannah didn't want to look at all. She knew the policeman was watching her, but she walked as slowly as she could across the almost empty room. The bright, white light disinfected every corner, daring a spider or a speck of dust to cloud the slippery, shining floor.

'Well?' It was cold in the room but drops of sweat oozed from the wrinkles in the policeman's fat face.

The body on the table was covered in a green sheet that was hard and rough from hundreds of harsh washings.

Hannah touched the sharp edge of the sheet and found herself thinking, 'Mama wouldn't have wanted to sleep in a hard sheet like that.' She thought herself out of the cold room as she remembered how she used to creep into her parents' bed on a Sunday morning and how soft and warm it was. And every Sunday her mother and father had laughed at her and told her she was too big to cuddle up in bed with her parents. Then they had moved over and made room for her and they were all warm together in the big, soft bed.

Hannah was freezing, but she didn't want to let the policeman see her shivering. They would have to keep the room cold, she thought. If they kept bodies in there. She didn't want to look at the woman on the narrow table, but the policeman was watching her. Even when he turned his back on her and pretended to shuffle through the papers on the grey metal desk near the door, she knew he was watching her. She didn't look, didn't want to look, at the dead woman. Papa had warned her that Mama had been badly injured and that there might be cuts and bruises on her face. Hannah didn't want to see all that, but it had to be done. All she had to do was identify the body and get out of there.

The policeman walked slowly over to the table. The hard, white light flattened his fat, white face, making his nose spread into his cheeks. 'Well?' he said. 'There's other people waiting. I've got other people to show, you know.'

Then Hannah went up to the end of the table and quickly pulled back the rough green sheet. Her mother's face was white, too. But she was always pale and white. Her eyelashes were white blonde, not as dark as usual, and Hannah realized they had washed her mother's face and taken off her make-up, like she always did before she went to sleep. Her left hand was crossed over her chest, touching her collarbone. Hannah felt sure she was asleep. While she watched the body she was sure she saw her chest rise and fall, rise and fall, as if Mama were still breathing.

Someone had taken Mama's long, blonde hair and coiled it in a plait that hung over her left shoulder. Hannah knew her mother would never have worn her hair in a plait like that. She wanted to shout, 'I've never seen this woman before in my life.' And she hadn't. She hadn't ever seen her mother like that. She wanted to know who had been touching her mother. They had no right to. Who had combed her hair after they brought her in to the police station and plaited it so that she looked like a princess from a fairy tale?

Someone had phoned to tell Hannah's father. That was when Papa had told her she would have to go with him to the building behind the police station. He hadn't said that if she didn't go, the secret police, the Stasi, would come and get her anyway. Instead, he'd told her not to be too afraid. He'd stroked Hannah's hair and said that in spite of her injuries Mama probably wouldn't look too bad. He said they always tried to make dead people look nice.

Hannah hadn't expected Mama to look so beautiful. She knew her mother woudn't have liked them doing her up so she looked like a fairy princess, but she couldn't say anything. Her shoulders ached because she wanted to hold Mama's hand. She had to force her hands to stay rigid by her side. Papa had told her not to touch anything. And she wasn't supposed to cry. Her shoulders ached and her throat ached and she wanted to lie close to Mama and feel her warm heart beating. Hannah told herself she was being a baby, but she felt like crying and she wanted her mother's arms around her.

The policeman's voice cut off her crying. 'Well?'

Hannah looked straight at him, not crying, not crying. He was sitting down again at his cold, metal desk, puffing and panting from the effort of walking round the room. 'Is this woman your mother?'

Hannah said, 'Yes.' Then she pulled the green sheet gently back over Mama's face and walked over to the policeman's desk. The room had an echo like an enormous cavern, deep underground.

'Then you'll have to answer a few questions. It won't take long. I have other people to show. And your father'll have to take a look, before we settle the case.' He flapped a fat, white hand in the direction of a metal folding chair against the wall opposite his desk, but Hannah didn't want to sit down. The policeman shrugged his shoulders and took a form out of the drawer. Name? Address? Relationship to the deceased?

Hannah knew what to say. Her voice was calm and steady. She told the policeman that she hadn't seen her mother for six months. 'She didn't want to live with us any more,' Hannah said. 'So she moved out. I don't know where she was, but my father must have known because she still got letters at our house. He sent them on to her.'

The policeman's eyes were another wrinkle in his fat face. 'You mean you never saw her at all? The whole of the last six months?'

Hannah looked down at the slippery, stone-cold floor. Flecks of grey glimmered like silver ore in the green stone. 'She didn't want to live with us any more.'

'And weren't you upset about that?'

Hannah looked up at the ceiling and the bright, white light stung her eyes. 'I still had my father. We couldn't force my mother to stay with us, could we?'

The policeman grunted. 'Well, she wasn't registered anywhere else. The address we've got in our records is the same as yours.'

Hannah stared at the man's hands, lumps of white fat, delicately holding his sharpened pencil. 'I don't know. She was with her friends, I suppose.'

'Don't mumble down at the ground.' The man tapped on the table with his pencil. 'Now, you say she had a boyfriend . . .'

Hannah shook her head. She knew he was trying to get her to cry, or to say something she hadn't planned to say. 'She just didn't want to live with us. And she knew she'd have to wait a long time for a new flat of her own. So she lived with friends. How should I know where she was?'

Every time the policeman stopped writing, he tapped with his pencil on the flat of his hands. Hannah kept her eyes on the pencil. 'She must have told you about her plans to go over the Wall to the West.'

4

Hannah put her hands behind her back and squeezed her shoulders together, trying to stop them aching. 'She didn't want to live with us. I haven't seen her for six months. Perhaps longer. How should I know what she was going to do?'

'So,' said the policeman. 'Your mother moved away to live with someone you don't know in a place you've never been to. You didn't hear from her for six months, and now you've come to see what happens to people who are foolish enough to betray our Socialist Fatherland by trying to go over the Wall to the West, instead of putting in an official application? Is that everything?' He lifted up the paper to see if his writing had gone through the carbon and made a good copy of the form. 'If that's all you've got to say for yourself, I may as well have your father in now.'

'I only came here because they said I had to,' Hannah said. 'It wouldn't have bothered me if I'd never seen her again.'

But it wasn't like that.

She had last seen her mother the day before. And she hadn't really moved out of their house. All her things were still there. But for some reason, Hannah's parents wanted people to think they'd broken up, so her mother stayed with her friend, Dorle.

Mama and Papa had talked for years about moving to West Germany. Almost every month something happened at Mama's school that made her come home furious. She would throw her bag on to a chair and throw herself on to the sofa with a, 'Right! That's it! That's the limit! This country can't get any worse for me now.'

The certificates made her get really angry. Every time it came round to the end of term or the end of a school year, Mama would talk about children who were good at their school work and still hadn't been given their Certificates for Good Work in the Socialist School. If her pupils didn't want to join the Young Pioneers, or if their parents weren't in the

Party, the teachers were expected to give them lower marks or not to award them a Certificate—even if they had the best marks in the whole class.

And then there was the time when all those pupils were expelled from Mama's school. Hannah never found out why.

Her mother said, 'You don't need to know about such things.' But Hannah wanted to know. For weeks, her mother used to come home from work and shut herself up in the bedroom. Hannah knew she was crying. Every day, she asked, 'What's the matter, Mama?' and the answer was always the same.

'It's not important. It won't do you any good to know about such things.'

Hannah's mother and father talked late at night, after Papa came home from the theatre and Hannah had been in bed for at least three hours. They didn't know she couldn't sleep. And even though the bedroom door was always closed, Hannah heard her mother shouting and crying. That was how she knew about the six pupils who had been expelled. She heard her mother sobbing:

'No. No. They hadn't done anything wrong. They weren't caught smoking. They hadn't been stealing or bullying. They were some of my brightest pupils. And they worked hard. What they did wasn't wrong!' Then she lowered her voice.

Hannah climbed down the ladder from her platform bed and crept over to her parents' bedroom, putting her head close to the door, trying to hear what they were saying. But she never got to hear what the pupils had done to get themselves expelled. She thought there were four boys and two girls, but she wasn't sure.

All she knew was that Mama had been off work for a month after they were expelled, even though Hannah couldn't see that there was anything wrong with her. Her mother kept going to see the doctor and saying he'd told her to stay at home for another week. She was happy as long as she stayed at home, but she couldn't stay off work for ever.

After her mother went back to work, Hannah's parents got

careless and started talking about the Wall in front of her. It was as if she wasn't there. Sometimes they had huge rows, but most of the time they just talked quietly about what would happen if the family moved away. Hannah always knew what they were talking about, even when they tried to use code words so she wouldn't understand. Sometimes they talked in English, because Hannah was learning Russian at school. But if people talk about the same thing often enough, it's easy to understand what they're saying, whatever language they speak.

After the pupils were expelled from her mother's school, Hannah's parents hardly talked about anything else. She wondered whether other people's parents went on and on about moving to West Germany. But she knew it wasn't safe to ask.

Everyone watched West German TV. And the kids in her class talked about what it must be like in the West, out in the playground, when there were no teachers around. Some of them dreamed of going to the West because you could buy dozens of different cars there. In the West, you didn't have to put your name on a waiting-list and wait ten years for a car. And you didn't have to pay thousands and thousands of marks for a tiny Trabant that was only big enough for two and a half people. People said that in the West, you could go into a showroom, point to the car you wanted, put your money on the table, and drive it home.

Hannah didn't really believe all that. On East German TV, she watched films about the people with no jobs in West Germany, about drug addicts and the teenagers who went out on the streets selling drugs because their families were so poor. At least everyone in the East had a job.

It wasn't that Mama believed everything they saw on West German TV. She wasn't interested in cars. She just used to get mad about the school where she taught and kept saying that she knew the schools must be fairer in the West.

Papa didn't really think her mother should put up with the way things were at school. But when they argued, he always

7

said it wasn't right to run away. He said that if she thought the schools were so bad, she should stay in the East and try to make them better. As far as Hannah could tell, her parents still loved each other. They just couldn't agree about where to live.

They were obviously planning something. About six months before Hannah's mother was killed, her parents suddenly told her she should tell all her friends that they were splitting up and that Mama was moving out. They didn't say why. They just said it was important. And they said Hannah was the only one who would know their secret, that they still loved each other. They even told Oma and Opa, on the phone to Leipzig, that Mama was moving out to live with a friend.

But they still saw Hannah's mother every day. And when they went to visit Hannah's grandparents in Leipzig for Christmas, Mama came too. Hannah thought it was all a bit stupid. She was tired of telling lies and now she even had to lie to her best friend, Sabina. She knew that everyone had to lie, that it was dangerous, sometimes, to tell the truth, but she was tired of it. She didn't see why they had to make up even more lies for her to tell.

Whenever her Form Teacher, Frau Bruck, said something like, 'If you can't manage this homework on your own, ask your mothers to help you,' she had to put her hand up and say, 'Please, miss, my mother doesn't live with us any more.'

Hannah couldn't remember when she had learned that it was important not to tell everyone at school what your family was doing. It must have been some time when she was very, very small. She felt she had always known that school was a place where you didn't tell the whole truth. But Hannah had always told Sabina everything. That was the worst part, not being allowed to tell the truth to her best friend.

When Hannah told them her mother had moved away, everyone at school was really kind to her. She felt terrible. Someone called a meeting of the whole class and talked about how bad she must be feeling and how everyone would have to help her. Paul Sehr stood up and told them, for the tenth time, how bad he had felt when his father went on a visit to the West and never came back. His father hadn't even written to them since he left. Paul gave Hannah his phone number and told her to call him if she felt like talking. The others put their arms round her and told her they'd look after her.

Hannah felt like a snake. For weeks, Frau Bruck was extra helpful with her schoolwork. Every time Hannah made a mistake in maths, Frau Bruck would murmur, 'You've got a lot to think about at the moment.' Paul Sehr brought her bars of chocolate.

And all the time, Mama was still living close to them, at Dorle's house. Hannah went there when she got home from school, because her mother's school finished earlier.

Hannah never imagined that life could be any different. The time after she got home from school was always the nicest part of the day. They all ate their evening meal together with Mama and Dorle and her husband. Papa was usually there for an hour or two before he had to go out to the theatre and Hannah walked back to the flat with him. She didn't mind staying on her own in the flat as long as she knew her mother was so close. If Hannah couldn't do her homework, Mama was always there to help. That was why she felt so guilty when Frau Bruck and Paul Sehr wanted to help her as well.

Sabina made Hannah feel guilty too. Hannah couldn't understand how her mother could deceive Sabina's mother. They'd been friends since before Hannah was born, and now her mother was acting as if Sabina's mother didn't exist. Sabina kept saying, 'It must be awful for you, now your mama's gone,' and her parents invited Hannah to go to their flat after school, so she wouldn't be lonely. Hannah hated herself for all the lies she told. She had to pretend she had jobs to do for her father. People were so kind for the first month or two after Mama was supposed to have gone away. But then the fuss gradually died down.

It was only after they shot Hannah's mother that she

9

realized why her parents had made her tell all those lies and pretend that her mother had moved out and left them. It was so that Hannah wouldn't get put in a home.

Hannah was angry about that. If they'd told her what her mother was planning to do, she would have known straight away why she was supposed to keep up the pretence about her mother leaving. Everyone in Hannah's street knew about the Schell family. Both parents had tried to get over the Wall, taking their children with them. Hannah knew all about it because Mechthild Schell was in the class below her at school. Everyone felt sorry for the children after it happened.

Mechthild's father was a scientist, and they drove out into the country and tried to escape with another family. They sewed a hot-air balloon out of old sheets and dresses and anything else they could get their hands on. At least, that was what people said, people who had seen the report on West TV. Hannah never saw it. What she wanted to know was how they managed to hide the balloon while they were making it, because they only lived in a flat like Hannah's. Mama said they probably kept the balloon covered up on their allotment. They'd waited years to get an allotment out near Potsdam.

Anyway, they had been really stupid. They tried to float over the Wall in their balloon. Even though they tried to do it at night, they must still have known how many guards there were all along the border, with all those floodlights out, and Alsation dogs on no-man's land. The balloon was shot down before they got anywhere near the Wall. Hannah knew she wouldn't even have heard about it if Mechthild hadn't been at her school. They didn't put things like that in the papers.

The balloon landed in no-man's land in front of the Wall and some of the girls said that Mechthild's brother got bitten by one of the Alsation dogs they used to patrol the land. Hannah didn't know about that. All she knew was that the four grown-ups were put in prison and the children were put in children's homes. And the School Director told them that always happened when families were caught trying to escape. Except that he didn't say they were caught trying to escape:

he said they were caught betraying their Socialist Fatherland. The children were taken away and put into homes because their parents weren't fit to bring up children in a Socialist state. And some people said that even when the parents were released from prison, they were never allowed to have their children back again.

After they shot Mama, Hannah knew straight away that if her father pretended he had no idea what her mother had been planning to do, she wouldn't get put in a home. That's why she knew what to say to the policeman when they made her go and identify the body. And that was why she didn't cry, or touch her mother's hand. She didn't want to be taken away from Papa as well and put in a children's home. And Papa didn't deserve to be put in prison.

That was why she stood there in that cold room, with Mama lying dead on the table, and pretended she didn't care.

When they got home from the police station, her shoulders were aching from sitting in another room with a policewoman watching her, waiting for hours while Papa went in to look at the body. She had been forced to sit there with her shoulders sort of hunched up, trying to look like people look when they are bored and don't care about anything very much. And she had an ache in her throat from not crying. Even after they got home, she didn't want to cry in front of Papa, because she thought it would upset him even more. Hannah didn't want to upset him.

Hannah needed to talk about Mama, but not to Papa, because that might have made him cry. She had a headache all the time and she knew there was only one way to get rid of it. More than anything, she wanted to tell the truth. She'd had enough of telling lies.

She wanted to tell Sabina and the others at school, and Frau Goetz in the flat across the way from their flat, that Mama hadn't left them after all. She wanted to tell everyone that her mother never meant to leave them really. And she wanted people to understand that her parents still loved each other, that it wasn't like they had said for six months. She was desperate to tell the truth, but her grandparents were the only people she could really trust, and they were hundreds of miles away in Leipzig. And now it wasn't only the long journey which separated her from Oma and Opa; no one had forced them to look at the body in that large, cold room with its high, white walls. They were not trapped, like Hannah.

The phone rang soon after they got back from the police station. Papa sighed and looked a bit relieved as he went to answer it. Hannah got the feeling he didn't like being alone with her in their small living-room without Mama. She already felt as if she was in the way.

As soon as her father started talking, Hannah knew it was Oma on the phone. If he was speaking to someone at work, Papa always used the kind of German they taught at school. But with her grandparents he relaxed and spoke like he always did in Leipzig.

He didn't have much to say. And he didn't mention Mama. They had agreed months before not to talk about Mama on the phone. Papa and Mama were always saying things like, 'You never know who might be listening.' Hannah had done what she was told, even though she thought they were stupid to believe that there were people listening in to every phone call she made. But she was shocked at her father's silence. He had just seen her mother dead in that cold, white room and still he said nothing.

'Oma wants to talk to you.' Papa gave the phone to Hannah and went into the kitchen. The door slammed shut behind him, so that she didn't hear the first thing Oma said. But Hannah had a feeling that her grandmother knew about Mama. She was scared she would break down and cry and tell Oma all about it, even though they had agreed not to talk about Mama on the phone. The room where her mother lay, with its high, white walls and the policeman watching her, watching her, would not go away. It was a prison wrapping its walls around her wherever she went. She wasn't free to say what she felt, not even to Oma.

She said Hallo. She never said very much when Oma was on the phone, mainly because her grandmother talked so much. She always told Hannah what she'd cooked for dinner and where she'd been and what her friends had done and who she'd visited in hospital. And because they were all people Hannah had never met, she usually just said, 'Mm. Yes. Nice.' And Oma never seemed to mind.

This phone call was different.

Oma said, 'Hallo, my little girl! How are you?'

Hannah said she was fine. Oma's voice was the same as always, bright and cheerful. She was always excited and happy about something. But Hannah knew that she knew about Mama. The silence at the other end of the line asked awkward questions until Hannah thought she'd better say something. 'It was really sunny at the weekend, Oma.' It wasn't like Oma to be so quiet. 'It was so hot that we went to the Alexanderplatz. Papa and me. We sat on the steps in the sun and had ice-cream.'

'Yes. It was warm here, too, on Sunday.' Oma waited for her to say something again. Hannah wanted to put the phone down. Instead of their living-room, she saw the policeman, watching and listening to every word she said, from the room with its high, white walls. What did Oma expect her to say? All Hannah could think of was Mama sitting on the steps in the Alexanderplatz and taking off her jacket because it was so warm, and then jumping up and running over to the café to get them all an ice-cream.

Hannah realized she was pressing the telephone hard against her left ear so that it hurt. 'It only turned cold suddenly yesterday evening,' she said. She could see the linden blossoms out on the trees, lime-green flowers against an icy blue sky.

'Yes. We felt the cold too. Opa went to bed early. As soon as he got home.'

Hannah's throat starting aching again. She thought

13

perhaps she was getting a cold from the cold weather. 'It's started snowing today, Oma,' she said. 'The sky keeps on throwing down huge, great soft snowflakes like feathers. And then it stops and the sun comes through again. It's weird.'

'That's April weather for you,' said Oma. 'You know what they say. In April the weather does what it wants. Anything can happen.'

2
STEFFI
Berlin, October 1988

Steffi had had enough of keeping her mouth shut. She knew
they weren't supposed to sign petitions. She knew the
Director of her school had told them it wasn't safe to meet up
in large groups unless they were taking part in a Pioneer
meeting. But she had had enough.

She had had enough of writing essays which said that the
DDR was a peace-loving country, when she knew that wasn't
true. She had had enough of marching to the centre of Berlin
with the rest of her class and being forced to cheer for ancient
foreign presidents she had never even heard of, waving a
paper DDR flag in one hand and the visitor's flag in the
other. She had had enough of her teachers telling her that all
pollution and all wars and all drug addiction came from the
West. They thought she was stupid and she wasn't.

Someone had been putting up posters in her school
cloakroom, posters which disappeared almost as soon as they
were put on the wall. The posters said that there were too
many tanks and too many soldiers in the DDR. They called
for a peace demonstration. One poster read, 'Let's melt down
our weapons. Let's turn swords into ploughs for the fields.'

Steffi went along to one of the meetings. There weren't
many kids there and most of them were from the higher
classes. Two or three pupils came from Steffi's year. They all
signed the letter to the General Secretary of the Communist
Party, Erich Honecker, asking him to get rid of DDR tanks
and soldiers and work for peace. They all knew that they
weren't supposed to sign petitions.

They never held another meeting. The day after it
happened, pupils who had gone to the meeting were kept in

their classrooms all day and not allowed to talk to each other. Then they were shadowed when they went home.

The day after Steffi signed the letter, her mother took her up to the attic bedroom in their house, crept over to the window, lifted up a corner of the curtain and told her to peep out carefully so that no one from outside would see her. There was a man standing at the corner of their street, a young man with short, blond hair. He had one hand in his trouser pocket and the other on a small shoulder-bag he was carrying. He was slim and wore a short, zip-up leather jacket and jeans. When they first looked out he was looking in the opposite direction, but every five minutes he looked at his watch, pretended to turn round casually and glanced at their house.

'Stasi,' her mother said. 'Secret police. They all look like that, Steffi.'

'Just looks the same as anyone else to me,' said Steffi.

Her mother smiled. 'You'll soon be able to tell one.' She ran her hand through Steffi's mop of long, brown, curly hair. 'You've got to laugh at them, really. Secret police and they can't even keep themselves secret.' She let the curtain down. 'At least we haven't got a phone for them to bug. They've never stopped bugging me at work ever since your father left. But I've got used to that.' Then she said, 'I'm proud of you, Steffi. You're stupid and you never listen, but I'm proud of you for standing up for what you believe in. This country would be a better place if more people did that.'

Steffi shrugged her shoulders. 'All I did was sign a petition.'

Her mother said, 'They're going to give you a hard time, you know. They probably won't let you join the FDJ.'

'Oh, cool!' Steffi grinned. 'I never wanted to, anyway.'

Steffi's mother had to go and speak to the School Director. He told her that Steffi had been led astray by older children who should have known better. That evening, she arrived home late with the new box of water colours she needed for her work. The shop had finally got some in after she had been waiting for ten weeks. And on the way home she had passed a vegetable shop where she had joined a big queue of people. She didn't know what they were queueing for, but it looked as if it must be something good because the queue was so long. The people at her end of the queue didn't know what was at the other end either. It was only when the queue started to move and people came out of the shop that Steffi's mum saw they were selling peaches. And she was lucky enough to get four of the last ones. Peaches in winter. She was in a good mood when she got home.

They sat down at the kitchen table and she started to cut the peaches up with a sharp knife. Steffi took half a peach and the juice ran down her chin as she bit into it. 'Mmm. OK, what did he say, Mama?'

Her mother smiled and pretended to be shocked at the great slurping noises Steffi was making in between bites of peach. 'He said you're not going to be punished, but that the older pupils are going to face the severest penalty, whatever that is. He said you younger ones were led astray and the fifteen-year-olds should have known better.'

Steffi sat down. The kitchen table had dark knots in each plank and she ran her finger round and round one of the dark patches, following the grain of the wood. Her mother cut the last peach up into slices and pushed the blue enamel plate towards her, but Steffi didn't look at the fruit. Round and round her finger went on the smooth wood and then she changed direction. 'That's not fair,' she said, hitting the rough centre of the knot with each word. 'Nobody led me astray. I can think for myself, you know.'

Her mother shrugged her shoulders. She stood up and tied her hair into a loose pony-tail before she went over to the sink and started to peel potatoes. 'At least they aren't going to punish you.'

Steffi didn't want to go to school any more. She started to feel sick in the mornings when she woke up because she didn't want to face the atmosphere at school. She didn't know who she could trust. It wasn't that someone had told on them;

17

they had all signed their names on the letter for the whole world to see. They had wanted to show what they believed in.

No. What made Steffi feel sick was the way the other kids in her class avoided anyone who had signed the petition. Boys who had complained just as much as they had about the fact that everyone had to join the army when they left school, pretended not to know them. As if the ones who had written a letter to Erich Honecker, the most important man in their country, had some kind of infectious disease.

On the day she had signed the petition, Steffi had been absolutely sure that every one of her classmates agreed with her. Whenever they got together at lunchtime, all of them said they had had enough of the army and of the stupid lies their teachers told them. And now they were telling lies too, and looking at the floor or the ceiling every time they passed Steffi in the corridor. Steffi felt sick every day, but her mother wouldn't let her stay at home. 'It'll all blow over,' she said. 'They'll all forget about it in a month or two.'

But it didn't all blow over. Steffi saw men who looked like Stasi in the school corridors. Now they weren't content with following people home. For weeks, they were snooping round the school, asking questions, even interviewing some of the petitioners in the Director's office. Steffi wasn't called to the Director, but she couldn't work. Her form teacher scolded her for day-dreaming, but Steffi couldn't concentrate. She felt sick all the time and she lost weight because she couldn't eat. She wanted to talk to some of the older pupils, the fifteen-year-olds who kept being called into the Director's office and being interviewed, but she was never allowed to get anywhere near enough to talk. She only saw them as they walked to their lessons. Everyone whispered when they talked about what the Director might have meant when he said they would face the severest penalty.

Steffi hated the Director, with his thin, dyed black hair. And she began to hate all the teachers. She hated them for carrying on with their lessons as if everything was normal when all she wanted to do was to talk about what had happened. She wanted to ask them what was so wrong about signing a petition asking for peace. Before she had signed, she was aware that there were two kinds of teacher in her school. There were those who were so loyal to the Party that they would tell their classes black was white if the Party told them to. And then there were the other teachers who would stick their necks out and sometimes tell the class their own opinions as well as the Party opinions they were supposed to teach.

But after Steffi had signed the petition, it felt as if the teachers had all become robots, all repeating the same words because someone else was pressing the button that controlled their speech. Even their art teacher, who always chatted to them during the lessons as if they were friends, became quiet and serious and said, 'No talking. I think it's best if we get on with our work without talking today.' Steffi felt sick at the way they stopped her from talking.

The whole school was gripped with fear, like people in a city who have been warned that a hurricane is about to strike. And it was as if someone had told them that if they didn't talk about the wild wind, if they pretended it wasn't howling around outside, it would go away and leave them to carry on their lives as before.

Then one day, the Director called a special assembly. Their school was one of the best in Berlin, so an extra large picture of Erich Honecker grinned down at them from above the stage. When Steffi's class marched into the hall, the first three classes were already standing silently in a semi-circle, one class behind the other. The teachers went to sit on the stage. All of them sat upright and stared at the far wall with its memorial to the victims of Fascism and militarism, former pupils who had fallen in the Second World War. Steffi's art teacher was the only one who leaned forward in her chair, with her head on her knees. It looked as if she was about to faint, but no one paid any attention to her.

The oldest pupils came in last and stood in a line right in front of the Director. Steffi turned round and looked up at the balcony behind her. Two men who didn't belong in the school sat right at the back, staring down at the pupils and teachers with eyes like binoculars. She thought of what her mother had said: 'What's the good of a secret police who can't even keep themselves secret?' But she didn't feel like smiling. She wondered if she would actually be sick or whether she was just going to feel awful until the whole special assembly was over. No one said a word.

Then the Deputy Director read out the names of three boys and two girls in the upper class. Steffi recognized the five who had first started the petition and had the idea to send it to Erich Honecker. The Director called out the first on his list: 'Christina Oloff'.

Christina stepped forward and looked straight at the Director. She had her arms folded in front of her chest and looked impatient, as if she had something much more interesting to do than stand about listening to him. The Director was scared to look her in the eye. 'You have brought shame on your school and on the Socialist State,' he said. Then he raised his right hand, still holding the piece of paper with the names on and pointed at the door. 'Go.' Christina glared at him and then smiled at her classmates. None of them smiled back at her, their friendship frozen by the presence of the Stasi. Then she walked quickly out of the room.

In turn, the Director called out each of the five and ordered them to leave the school. Thomas Amsel couldn't take the strain of waiting. He was the last one to be called, and collapsed as the Director read out the accusation against him. Two teachers carried him out of the hall, holding on to his arms as if he were a prisoner. Steffi could still hear Thomas weeping as they dragged him along the corridor to the main entrance. She felt as if she would always hear the sound of Thomas weeping, the sound of his feet dragging along the polished red-tiled corridor.

'I have nothing more to say,' said the Director. 'Except that we have felt it necessary to issue a warning to the following pupils. They have been very, very lucky. This time, they will not face expulsion.' He started to read from a list of pupils from several classes and Steffi knew that her name was on the list too. But before he got to her class, she stepped forward.

'Stop, please.'

She was aware of teachers moving around the stage and of her classmates suddenly breaking their silence. She couldn't see what the two men on the balcony were doing and she didn't care. Out of the corner of her eye, she noticed her art teacher standing up and then being made to sit down again.

The Director was a thin, nervous man. His dyed black hair shone with hair-cream and his thin, grey face gleamed with perspiration so that it looked as if he was made of tin. Like a tin man, he looked as if he ought to have a large key in his back, so that at any moment someone could come up and turn the key, and he would walk off in the direction they sent him. He didn't know how to react to Steffi.

'I am ashamed of this school,' said Steffi. She had never spoken in the school hall before and she was surprised at how clear her voice sounded. She knew that everyone could hear her. 'And I am ashamed of the Socialist State for treating people like you've just treated my friends.' The Director raised his right arm as if someone had turned the key, too late, to set him in motion, but he didn't say anything. His hand went into his pocket and he took out a clean, white handkerchief and mopped at his cheek and his neck. 'I don't think I'm lucky to stay here,' said Steffi. 'I'm going.'

Steffi didn't see what happened after she left the hall. She didn't see the art teacher fainting and the Director's grey face turning purple as pupils and teachers all began to talk at once. She didn't hear the Director's voice strained to a high-pitched squeak when he tried in vain to speak above the noise and get everyone to listen to him. She walked quickly down the corridor and ran home, so quickly that even her shadow didn't know where she had gone.

Steffi tried hard to find out what had happened to the other kids from her school, but no one would tell her. None of the five who were expelled had really been her friends; they were in different classes and she had no idea where they lived. She kept thinking she would bump into one of them on the streets one day, but it was as if they had completely disappeared. Steffi saw other people from her school, but they didn't talk to her. After a month she moved to a new school and her mother told her to forget all about what had happened.

But Steffi couldn't forget. She would never forget the coldness of the Director's voice as he read out the charges against the ones who were about to be expelled. Two images of her School Director were scratched on her brain and kept on scratching and irritating her, as the images disappeared and then re-emerged, engraved on her mind. One image was in colour, a picture of the Director with a funny bowler hat, at their school fancy dress party the year before. Dressed up as Charlie Chaplin, he was, and he had even done Charlie Chaplin's funny walk across the stage for the party. The other image was black and white and the Director, in a black suit, with his right arm raised as if to strike someone, was frowning at Thomas Amsel, the last boy to be expelled.

Steffi couldn't forget the way they had dragged Thomas out of the school, the way her art teacher had slumped over her chair. She couldn't forget the Stasi men, stupid men trying to hide themselves in the gallery above the hall. Steffi had decided that in the DDR you could do one of two things: you could do what all her old classmates had done—behave as if you were stupid and let them tell you all sorts of lies and pretend you believed them, so you just might have a chance of getting a good job. Or you could speak the truth and perhaps end up doing the work no one else wanted to do. Steffi had had enough of lies.

She had already been asked to leave her second school, five months later, when her mother found out what had happened to Steffi's art teacher.

Steffi had nearly finished cooking the dinner by the time

her mother got home from work. The back door slammed shut as her mother dropped her bags of groceries and workbooks on the table. 'Mm. That smells good.' Her mother's voice was bright and full of life, but her face looked tired. She sat down, put her elbows on the table and pressed her fingers on her eyes, leaving white fingerprints when she took them away and smiled wearily at Steffi.

'What was your art teacher called, the one you said was almost collapsing the day you walked out of school?'

Steffi told her. She poured beaten eggs over the potatoes she had fried and reached up to get the blue plates out of the top cupboard.

'I thought that was her name. It must be the same person.'

'What's up? Has she tried to sell a painting to your boss?'

'She tried to drive through a border crossing and they shot her.'

Steffi took a knife and poked at the omelette. Her mother always told her not to do that, but she liked to make holes in the omelette and watch the still liquid egg get caught in the holes and turn solid.

'You're scratching the pan.'

'Look, who's doing the cooking today? You or me? Do it yourself if you don't like the way I cook.' Steffi switched off the gas and threw the knife down. It fell into the gap between the cooker and the old china cupboard.

Her mother got up and picked up the knife. 'It happened a week ago, Steffi. I'm sorry. I know you liked her.'

'I'd forgotten all about her,' said Steffi. 'I don't even remember what she looked like. I'd forgotten all of them except for that vicious toad of a Director.' She took a spatula and started to ease the omelette on to a plate. 'Yours is done already,' she said, breaking pieces of potato out of the omelette and eating them with her fingers. 'I put it in the oven.' She sat down and started to shake salt over her omelette. 'None of the teachers ever did anything for us.'

'She must have been upset about it, though. I thought she was the one who was always really nice to you. You can't have forgotten her? She was one of the few honest teachers in that place.' Steffi's mother sat down. 'She was off school for weeks after the five were expelled. Then the doctor said she was OK, so she started back at work. And now she's dead. Just because she'd had enough of their lies. They shot her, Steffi.'

'I hadn't forgotten her,' said Steffi.

3
HANNAH
Berlin, April 1989

It was during the spring holiday when they shot Hannah's mother. So noone got to hear about it. It was better that way. That way there was nobody from school to come knocking at their door to say they were all very sorry, and Hannah didn't have to put on her act about not caring. Except in front of Papa. She could tell he was upset because he didn't say much. And because she didn't want to make him feel even worse, she didn't say anything either. She thought that if she didn't say anything about Mama he would forget her more quickly.

She didn't want to go back to school. After they shot her mother, Hannah felt too old to be still at school. Sometimes during the rest of the holiday, school just didn't seem important any more. At other times, Hannah didn't want to go because she was afraid of how she would feel when she got home from school and her mother wasn't there.

She didn't want to face everyone in her class. After they shot her mother, she finally knew what it feels like when your mother has gone away for good. All those months, she'd been trying to imagine what it must feel like and pretending to be upset because Mama was supposed to have left them. She knew she had got it all wrong. Hannah couldn't believe that no one had seen through her all that time. She had had no idea what it feels like when your mother suddenly isn't there any more. It was all just pretending, a sham. Why had no one found her out? She couldn't understand why Frau Bruck hadn't come up to her one day and said, 'I saw you laughing out in the playground. You wouldn't be laughing like that if your mother had actually left you. Aren't you going to tell me what's really happening?'

Hannah decided that when she did go back to school, she would have to try to act just the same as before. Even if she felt like screaming and crying she had to remember that she was supposed to have got over her mother going away. Her mother was supposed to have left six months before. There was nothing to do but laugh and keep quiet about it.

Hannah liked her teacher, but you never knew who you could trust—especially at school. Hannah wished she could have told Frau Bruck what had happened, especially when her teacher said, 'If you've ever got any problems at home, you can always come and talk to me about it.' But if Hannah talked to her and then she told someone else, they'd know that Papa knew about Mama trying to escape. And they'd take Hannah away from him and put her into a home. Hannah knew that whatever happened, when she got back to school, she just had to keep quiet.

The night after they had been at the police station, Hannah's father had to go out to the theatre and leave her on her own. When he asked Hannah if she wanted him to arrange for someone else to come and look after her, she snapped at him, 'I'm not a baby. I can look after myself.' She was thirteen years old and she was used to staying on her own when Mama went to meetings in the evenings.

But it wasn't the same.

It was different when Mama went out at seven and Hannah knew she'd be back at nine. It had been different when Hannah knew her mother was at Dorle's. She was used to her father not getting home until late. That was why he was always the one who got the breakfast and cleaned the house. He used to say he couldn't sleep very well after the theatre, so he had a short sleep and then slept again while Hannah and her mother were both out at school.

After they shot Hannah's mother, her father slept nearly all the time. Whenever he didn't have to be at work, he was sleeping. When he stopped making Hannah's breakfast, she didn't mind at all. She didn't feel much like eating anyway. But when her father noticed that she never had breakfast, he got

mad at her and said she was lazy. He said the only reason she didn't eat breakfast was that she was just too lazy to go and get it for herself. But it wasn't like that. Hannah didn't feel like eating. Papa didn't eat much either, but there was no one to shout at him.

Hannah was sick the day before school started and her father didn't even notice. She didn't want him to. She didn't want to bother him. He got up at breakfast time and came into the kitchen.

Their flat near the centre of Berlin, Hannah's home for as long as she could remember, was very small. Their kitchen was about the size of a large airing cupboard. Hannah couldn't remember the cooker they had once had because it had broken when she was small. Then they had waited and waited for one, and there was a different reason every month why they were all sold out before they even arrived in the showroom.

One day, a cooker had suddenly arrived, but after the man had gone and Hannah had helped her mother unpack it, they realized that it was a gas cooker. None of the flats in their block had gas. So the shop had taken it back and said they'd send another one soon. Two years had passed and Mama had grown tired of complaining.

That was one of the things she used to have arguments with Papa about. He used to tell her she just had to keep on at them if she wanted a cooker. 'You've got to be down there every day, pestering them, if you want them to do anything for you,' he used to say. 'Make sure they don't forget your face. Make yourself a nuisance. Then you'll get it soon enough.'

And Mama used to say she didn't want to spend her life rushing around to shops, pestering people about normal things every family needed. The thing that made her most angry was that she knew people who had got cookers much more quickly, because they had given the salespeople at the department store extra money for themselves, or a crate of wine. And that was one thing Mama said she wouldn't do. She said she wasn't going to bribe anyone. Papa would shrug

his shoulders and say, 'If that's the only way to get a cooker, I can't see what's wrong with it.'

When they couldn't get a proper cooker, Mama had bought one of those electric stoves which you can put two saucepans on, and a tiny grill that would do one piece of toast at a time. The grill was always breaking down, but Mama could get it to work because she had a bag of spare fuses Hannah's father had brought from the theatre.

After they had sent the cooker back, Hannah could see that a proper cooker wouldn't have fitted in their kitchen anyway. Mama never thought of that when she was getting so angry about it. But Hannah did. Their kitchen was so small that they probably wouldn't have been able to open the door of a cooker even if they had managed to get it into the room. When they had the first one delivered, the man just left it in the living-room and there it took up so much space that no one could reach the sofa to sit down.

As soon as Papa came into the kitchen, the day before Hannah started back at school, she went out again into the living-room. As usual, she didn't feel like eating. He was bound to shout at her.

'What's this?' He shuffled into the living-room, holding up the plastic bag of white, soggy bread for toasting.

'It's always going mouldy, Papa.' Hannah felt like throwing up. He'd picked out the piece of bread on the top and it was covered with grey-green furry stuff. 'Sometimes you can find a slice that's not mouldy further down.'

Her father whirled round and she heard him back in the kitchen shoving the whole bag of bread into the bin. Then he came and sat down beside her. Hannah's father wasn't very heavy, but the sofa sagged as soon as two people sat down on it. It was an old one they had got from Oma years before.

'We haven't got any milk,' he said.

'I know.'

'Don't you drink milk any more?'

'Not on its own.' Hannah had stopped drinking milk for breakfast when she was about six. She frowned. Papa got breakfast for them every day and now he couldn't even remember that she only liked milk in cocoa.

'You should drink milk,' he said. 'It's good for you. A growing girl like you.'

The thought of drinking milk made Hannah feel even sicker. She wanted to rush off to her bed and lie down. But she thought it would get him worried if she did that, so she stayed on the sofa. Her stomach was rolling like the clothes in a spin-drier.

'How long have we had that bread?' he asked.

'I don't know.'

But Hannah did know. Neither of them had been out to the shops for about six days, not since Mama had gone. They had hardly done anything. Papa had dragged himself out to work every night, coming home much earlier than usual. A few times, he had woken up at lunchtime and said he was going out for a breath of fresh air, but he never went. He just sat there on the sofa.

When he went out to work, he didn't take his bag with him. Hannah noticed that because she had never known her parents to go anywhere without their shopping bags. Nobody did. You never knew when you might come across something good for sale. If Hannah saw a queue anywhere when she was on her way home from school, she always used to run home and tell Mama or Papa. Then they would give her some money and she would go and stand in the queue. Most times, she didn't even know what was for sale, but everyone knew that it must be something good, something you couldn't usually get, if there was a queue.

One time, Hannah queued for hours and brought home some thin, green stuff called asparagus. She didn't think much of it, but Mama and Papa thought it was marvellous. They'd only ever eaten it once before and Papa said they had never seen it in the shops. Mama said bitterly that it was probably in the shops because of some atomic explosion in

29

Russia, but Hannah could never understand her when she talked like that.

In the DDR, people had to shop all the time. Mama said they were like the birds that spent their time pecking up thousands and thousands of grains every day to stay alive. People had to move from one shop to another, from one queue to another, to feed themselves. But for the last few days, Hannah and her father had forgotten those unwritten laws of survival. Hannah hadn't wanted to go shopping in case she met anyone from school. They were bound to ask her if she'd had a good time in the holidays and she needed time to prepare the lies she had to tell. And Papa just kept forgetting to buy what they needed.

He went back into the kitchen and Hannah heard him opening the two cupboard doors. Then he stood at the kitchen door with two glass jars in his hands. The stuff in the jars looked as fuzzy and green-grey mouldy as the bread, but Papa was grinning. 'How would you like pickled herrings and sour cucumbers for breakfast?'

4

Berlin, April 1989

A twig snapped in the grass behind Hannah and she whirled round. She must have looked annoyed, because the girl said:

'Is this bit of the playground private property or something? I mean, you've only got to say . . .' She looked as if she came from West Berlin. Her black leather jacket had long fringes on it, like people wore on the pop music shows on West TV. But her shoes gave her away. She was wearing the sort of trainers West German teenagers had had on two years before. And hers were made of plastic. Hannah knew that they came from the Central Department Store near Alexanderplatz, the big square they called the Alex.

Hannah had never seen the girl before and she didn't want to see her again. She resented her arriving new after the spring holidays and straight away making for Hannah's own secret place at the far side of the playground. It wasn't as if it really was secret. It was just that it was so far away from the main entrance to the school that nobody else ever went there. And Hannah needed to be alone. She had arrived at school specially early to see if being there would help her to work out what to say to Sabina.

'No. It doesn't belong to anyone.' Hannah put her hands in her pockets and hitched up her jeans. 'I just come here because I like to be alone sometimes.'

'Be like that!' The girl tramped off back towards the main entrance to the school, stopping only to kick a tree branch out of her way. Her hair was the orange colour of an almost ripe tomato and looked as if she had cut it herself with a blunt pair of scissors.

Hannah looked at her watch. It was twenty-past seven and the bell would be going at half-past. Sabina could walk into

31

the school gates at any moment and rush over to where Hannah was standing near the tree. They hadn't seen each other for ten whole days and they were normally so inseparable that everyone called them 'the twins'. Not that they looked like each other. Sabina had short black hair, while Hannah still wore her long, blonde hair in one tight braid which she'd learned to do herself. Hannah was much taller than Sabina, but they always wore similar clothes. Both of them had a pair of jeans from West Berlin, which Sabina's uncle had brought when he last visited them. Hannah hitched up her jeans again. She couldn't understand why they suddenly seemed too big for her.

Hannah saw Paul Sehr, standing right next to the front entrance. He always wanted to be first in the classroom—just like a kid in kindergarten. There was no danger of him coming over to disturb her near her tree when it was nearly time for the bell to go. She noticed the girl in the black leather jacket with fringes on it. Now she was kicking a football around with two kids from Class 5 who were mad on the game. Hannah's eyes followed the girl as she dribbled with the ball right up to Paul Sehr and then away from the door towards the gate. Then she kicked the ball back and strolled out of the school gate.

Hannah gasped at the girl's cheek and couldn't stop herself smiling two minutes later when the girl walked back in again. Still there was no Sabina. Hannah put her hands in her pockets and shivered. The wind tore at the trees and reminded Hannah of the row she'd had with Papa on her way out to school. He had told her she ought to wear a coat, and had run after her down the stairs waving her coat and shouting at her. As if she was still a baby in kindergarten.

Hannah didn't hear the bell ringing at first, but she saw Paul Sehr sprinting up the stairs of the main entrance and knew it was time to go in. For a split second, it occurred to her that Sabina might be ill. But Sabina was never ill. Hannah wondered, for the first time since school had finished for the spring holiday, why Sabina hadn't called her. She had been too preoccupied. Her mind had been imprisoned in that white-tiled room where she had seen her mother for the last time. Sabina could have called during the holidays, but then, she hadn't phoned Sabina either.

The playground had almost emptied and Hannah slid her top teeth over the bottom ones, frowning. If she ran she might not be late. But she didn't want to run.

Sabina was never late. Hannah knew she wouldn't turn up at school that day. At least she had one more day to think of what to say about her mother. She had one more day when she could practise the lies she had to tell, while she told all the others in her class. She imagined herself sitting with the whole class, sitting in the centre of a circle because Frau Bruck, their form teacher, always put them in a circle when they had something serious to discuss. Frau Bruck thought it was more relaxed that way. She used to say to the person in the centre of the circle, 'You can open your heart to us. Who on earth can you trust if you can't trust your own classmates?'

Hannah saw herself in the centre of the circle. She knew what Frau Bruck would say. 'Hannah is having difficulties in her family and we can all help by letting her talk about it.' That was what she had said six months before when Hannah's father had lied to her and paid a visit to school to tell her that Hannah's mother had left home.

Hannah reached the entrance to the school. A huge flight of grey stone steps swept upwards and one of the senior boys was standing at the top in his Free German Youth Party uniform. They were the worst, the ones who wore their FDJ uniform to school.

'My God, Hannah!' He wrote her name on a list he had attached to a clipboard. 'How have you managed to be five minutes late when I saw you arriving at school at ten-past seven?' He carefully screwed the top back on his fountain pen and attached the pen clip to his clipboard. Then he put his clipboard under his arm, his hands in the pockets of his baggy trousers and leaned nonchalantly against the stone urn at the top of the steps.

Hannah looked across the playground to the gate and then to the far end against the wall where there was a narrow strip of grass and some trees. It wasn't that far away. She couldn't explain why it had taken her five minutes to walk over from her tree to the entrance. So she shrugged her shoulders.

'I'd better get upstairs.'

The senior boy didn't hear her. He was already unclipping his pen from his clipboard. He carefully unscrewed the top and waited with his fountain pen ready to swoop on his victim as a small boy climbed the stone steps.

'You're late. Name?'

Hannah went inside. It would have been a nice building if it hadn't been a school. Slowly she climbed two more flights of stone steps, went past the Hall and past two classrooms, where she could hear the buzz of early morning class business through the open, frosted glass windows high up on the corridor wall of each room.

Hannah was ready to be shouted at. She didn't care. Her father had already told her she was stupid. What did it matter? She had never been late before, but she knew the kinds of things Frau Bruck said when kids came in late. 'Have you got an alarm clock? Yes? Then set it so it goes off fifteen minutes earlier tomorrow.' Being late would be marked on her report form and she would have to stay in for half an hour after school as well. But Hannah didn't care. Her father probably wouldn't notice she was late anyway.

She opened the classroom door.

'Sorry I'm late, Frau Bruck.'

Frau Bruck didn't shout. She didn't ask Hannah whether they had an alarm clock in their house. The chairs were already in a circle and she smiled at Hannah, just as the kindergarten teachers used to smile at the children when they were waking them from their afternoon nap. It was a careful sort of smile, as if she was carrying something fragile and she didn't want to drop it.

'Hallo, Hannah.' The words were gentle, but they made

Hannah's skin start to itch. 'We've all been waiting for you, my dear.'

It was just as Hannah had imagined it while she was standing out in the playground. She had imagined this scene in her classroom the whole week while she was at home, wondering what she would say about her mother lying there in the white-tiled room near the Stasi headquarters.

Frau Bruck put her arm gently on Hannah's shoulder and Hannah suddenly felt that pain again, that aching in her shoulders which had come when she held her hands tightly behind her back to stop herself reaching out and touching her mother's face.

'We may be a little late starting maths today.' Frau Bruck's face hardened for a second at the whispered cheers that hissed like steam from a pressure cooker. She pretended not to hear them but still she waited until there was dead silence. 'Hannah is having difficulties with her family,' she said. 'And we can all help her by giving her time to talk about it.' She sat down and patted the empty chair next to her in the circle. Hannah didn't like having to sit so close to Frau Bruck. When someone was sitting right next to you, you couldn't really look at them while you were talking to the whole class. But they could look at you. And watch you. And see if you were telling lies or not.

Hannah didn't say anything. Frau Bruck said, 'It's OK. Take your time.' But Hannah didn't want to say anything.

Paul Sehr was Pioneer Secretary for their class. They said he had been elected by the whole class, but everyone knew that wasn't true. Sabina had once gone round asking and no one had voted for Paul. Sabina said they had made him Pioneer Secretary because they felt sorry for him, with his father going off to the West. Paul's mother was still something important in the Party and Paul always carried the flag at Pioneer parades. Paul said, 'Does everyone know what has happened?'

Hannah didn't want him to tell them. It was none of their business, what had happened to her mother. But they always made it their business. They always talked like this when people had problems. When Paul's father had first gone away, they had talked about it. And since then they had talked and talked about how bad Paul felt because his father hadn't got in touch with them. When they were alone together, Sabina said she thought Paul had to make a big thing out of his father leaving, so his mother could carry on with her job in the Party. She said it wouldn't look good if Paul's family kept in touch with someone who had betrayed his country. But Hannah thought she was being a bit cruel. Anyone could see Paul was really upset, the way he broke down and cried in front of the whole class.

Hannah wasn't going to let them see her crying. And anyway, she hadn't cried when they first talked about her mother leaving home, so she didn't see how she could cry now.

Paul waited for Frau Bruck to say something. But she only nodded her head. Then she put her hand over Hannah's hand. That was the worst part. Hannah wanted to move her chair away, but Julia Gross was sitting very close to her on the other side, and Paul watched her from the opposite side of the circle of chairs, waiting to start.

Paul placed his two large hands on his knees and leaned forwards. He didn't look at Hannah any more. 'I don't know how many of you know about it,' he said. 'Hannah's mother died while she was trying to drive through the barriers at one of the border crossings.' He looked up at Frau Bruck for a second and then carried on. 'It was a terrible accident. The border patrol obviously thought it was terrorists.'

Frau Bruck nodded. 'They will, as usual, have issued two warnings,' she said. 'That's because the person or persons in the vehicle might have been teenagers who stole the car for a joyride and just didn't realize what they were doing.' Julia Gross gasped.

'I know that none of you would do a thing like that.' Frau Bruck smiled. 'But, unfortunately, there are teenagers who will do stupid things. Usually because of problems at home.'

She looked at everyone in the circle and smiled. 'That's why we talk things over, isn't it? We are all here to help each other.' She patted Hannah's hand again and then suddenly held it very tight. Hannah felt sick.

'The guards will definitely have issued two warnings.' Her grip tightened on Hannah's hand. 'And when Hannah's mother didn't stop, the border patrol shot at her tyres. They thought she was a terrorist, you see. A terrible mistake.' She shook her head. Hannah looked at Paul Sehr, who was searching the floor for spots of dust where there couldn't possibly be any spots of dust, because their classroom cleaning collective waged war on dust every morning before they started school. They all took turns doing the cleaning, and their cleaners' collective won the medal for the highest standards in the socialist school every year. But still Paul Sehr scanned the floor for specks of dust.

'It was an awful accident.' Frau Bruck squeezed Hannah's hand again and then took it and linked it with her left arm, still stroking Hannah's hand with her own right hand. Hannah pulled her hand away. 'They only ever shoot at people's tyres,' said Frau Bruck. 'That way, the driver of the car and anyone else they may be trying to kidnap and force to leave the DDR against their will, only sustain minor injuries. Obviously, they have to be questioned and sometimes imprisoned, but nobody would dream of killing them. As I say, they only shoot at the tyres and the car usually goes a little bit out of control.'

Hannah stared at Paul Sehr, but suddenly she didn't see him any more. She saw what she had refused to see when she was standing in the white-tiled room alone with her mother and the fat man from the border patrol. She had only pulled the rough, green sheet back for a short time and she remembered staring at the way they had arranged her mother's hair. But she had noticed something else before she placed the sheet back over her mother's face. Whoever had cleaned up the body had placed her mother's hand over her collar bone, so it was harder to see the patchwork of stitches and the bullet wound underneath. Hannah couldn't understand how she could suddenly remember so much about it. It was as if she had stood there for half an hour, counting the stitches, carefully examining what they had done to her mother. She had only been in the room for a short time.

Frau Bruck patted Hannah's hand again. Everyone was watching her. Hannah wished they would leave her alone. Only Paul Sehr was still looking at the ground, embarrassed. 'They shot at the tyres of the car Hannah's mother was driving, and the car went completely out of control, and hit against a concrete barrier. Hannah's mother was killed instantly.'

Everyone was quiet, still waiting for Hannah to say something, but words ricocheted round her brain like bullets from a machine gun. 'They didn't shoot the tyres. They shot her in the neck. They shot her in the chest.' And then, 'They didn't give her any warning.' Hannah knew that as well. No one had told her, but she knew. They hadn't given her mother any warning. She sat quietly and looked at Paul Sehr.

'Of course, what you've all got to realize is that it wasn't Hannah's fault.' Frau Bruck looked at each one of them in turn. 'Hannah really had nothing to do with this,' she said. 'And neither did her father. It was a decision her mother arrived at by herself. According to the school where her mother worked, she had been having difficulties lately, but she had refused to talk about them. She may have been ill. Hannah, did you want to say anything?'

Hannah didn't, but she thought they would leave her alone if she said something. So she said what she had heard herself saying, over and over again, in the week she had been on her own at home, wondering what she would say to everyone.

'I wish my mother hadn't done something so stupid.' She looked down at her black ankle boots. Her feet were hot and sweaty in them when she was indoors, and Papa had told her not to wear them to school. But they were the only shoes she had that went with her jeans. 'You don't have to worry about me, though. I mean, I can't say I feel all that bad. I hadn't even seen her for six months. It's very nice of you all to worry about me. I just wish she hadn't been so stupid.' Her classmates were gazing at her, like bloodsuckers trying to draw out of her what it feels like when your mother has just been killed. 'I suppose I feel a bit sorry for her.' Hannah looked at Frau Bruck to see if she was expected to say anything else.

'You're bound to feel bad about it, Hannah.' Julia scraped her chair backwards and Hannah could move a few centimetres away from her form teacher. Paul Sehr cleared his throat. His voice was breaking and he sometimes squeaked when he wanted to put on his deep, serious voice. 'I'd just like to say that we're all behind you, Hannah.'

Frau Bruck smiled and nodded. 'If ever you want to talk about it, let me know. After all, if you can't trust your form teacher, who can you trust?' Hannah never knew if she could trust Frau Bruck. And if you weren't sure, it was better not to trust anyone.

They began to clear the chairs away and put them behind the desks, placing the desk and chair legs precisely in the middle of the squares the cleaning brigade had painted on the floor, so that the desks always stood in an orderly line.

Then the door opened and slammed with an explosion that shook the panes of glass high up above the corridor. The girl Hannah had seen in the playground strode to the back of the class and sat down in Paul Sehr's place. She grinned at Frau Bruck.

'Sorry I'm late. I got lost.'

'Get on with your work now. Get on with your work.' Frau Bruck scuttled to the back of the classroom, where Paul Sehr was standing over the new girl, obviously trying to explain to her that she was sitting in his seat. Hannah heard the girl saying:

'Sorry! I wouldn't have sat here if I'd known it was private property,' before Frau Bruck led her to her own desk at the front of the classroom.

'I'm sorry to interrupt you again, boys and girls,' she said.

No one was working. Everyone was staring now at the new girl with her wild hair the orange colour of half-ripe tomatoes. Hannah was glad that no one was paying any more attention to her. 'Just before you get on with your maths, this is your new classmate, Stefanie Ahmed.' Someone repeated the foreign-sounding name, 'Ahmed?' Then Frau Bruck sat down with the girl and started writing things about her in the class record book.

Hannah looked at her watch. Their maths work was the same as every Monday. They were supposed to time themselves and see how many problems from their book they could do in an hour. But because they had had the class discussion about Hannah's mother, they now only had half an hour. Everyone was expected to work extra hard to make up for lost time. No one was talking. They were only ever allowed to talk when it was time for a class discussion, and then it was always the same people who did the talking.

Hannah looked at her watch. Five minutes had already gone and she realized she had spent the time staring at Sabina's empty place, three rows in front of her. None of the teachers ever allowed Hannah and Sabina to sit together, because they were such good friends. Hannah was glad Sabina was absent. She was glad she didn't have to see her on her first day back at school. She knew she would feel better about seeing Sabina after she had had a day of getting used to the others, making up stories that would convince them she hadn't really noticed her mother's disappearance. Hannah certainly didn't intend to tell them about going to the border police to identify the body. She would pretend her father had taken care of all that.

But Sabina was the one person Hannah really wanted to talk to. On the night they had come back home from the police station, Hannah had ached to go and talk to Sabina and tell her the truth, tell her everything that had happened for the last six months. She couldn't tell any more what hurt the most, whether it was her mother dying or having to tell lies to her best friend. It was all mixed up together, them killing her mother, and everyone telling lies all the time so that you didn't know who you could trust. Hannah ached to tell the truth. She had this idea that one day she would just walk around the Alex talking to complete strangers, policemen, tourists and families out shopping, saying, 'My mother tried to drive from East Berlin to West Berlin, so they shot her.' One day she would tell everyone what they had done.

But telling the truth was still a dream. Hannah knew she would never be able to tell the truth to anyone as long as she lived in East Berlin. Tomorrow, or whenever Sabina came back to school, she would have to lie to her and shrug her shoulders and tell her she hadn't seen her mother for such a long time that it didn't really make much difference whether she was alive or not. She hated the thought of telling lies to Sabina. Only the idea that Sabina could lie to her was worse. But Sabina wouldn't. Sabina would never lie to her. Hannah knew she could trust Sabina absolutely. She decided that one day, perhaps not tomorrow, she would tell Sabina everything. After that she felt much better.

At the end of the day, Frau Bruck asked Hannah to stay behind. That was only what Hannah had expected. She knew that people who were late for school had to stay in for half an hour. And she hadn't done her maths either. Hannah couldn't remember what she had done the whole day. Other kids had spoken to her and said they were sorry about her mother. And Hannah remembered saying, over and over again, 'Oh, it's not too bad, really. I got used to her being away.' But she didn't remember anything they did in their lessons. She couldn't even remember what teachers she had had that day. Whoever she'd had, they were bound to have complained about her, so she stayed at her desk and waited until the others had left the room and Frau Bruck strolled over.

She sat on the desk in the next row, swinging her legs. Hannah thought that she wasn't really as old as some people said she was. Julia Gross always said Frau Bruck was older than her grandmother, but Hannah could see that the teacher was probably the same age as her mother had been, about thirty-five. She just looked older because she wore very formal clothes.

'I've got more bad news for you, Hannah, I'm afraid.'

Hannah sat up straight and gripped the edge of her chair. 'I know,' she said. She thought Frau Bruck was going to tell her the truth they had concealed from the others, that her mother had been shot. She felt relieved. If Frau Bruck wasn't going to lie to her about that, perhaps she could be trusted.

'Did Sabina tell you?' Frau Bruck's eyes narrowed. 'I always thought she trusted me, but I never heard a thing about it until today, when the Director called me into his office. I must have looked a bit foolish.'

Hannah smiled at the idea that Sabina would ever have told Frau Bruck anything. 'I'm not that stupid,' Sabina used to say. 'Whatever you tell teachers, they use it against you.' But Sabina told Hannah everything. Hannah was confused.

'I must say, I was rather hurt when I found out,' said Frau Bruck. 'Sabina was such a nice girl. I expect it wasn't her fault. You see, everyone has problems with their families.'

Hannah didn't want to admit that she didn't know what Frau Bruck was talking about, so she nodded in agreement.

'No one seems to know whether they went via Czecho-slovakia or Hungary,' said Frau Bruck. She fiddled with a pile of maths books, turning round the ones with spines facing the wrong way.

'Hungary.' Hannah had no idea which border Sabina and her family had crossed to leave East Germany forever and live in the West. But she knew now that Sabina had gone and that Sabina had treated her in the very same way she had treated Frau Bruck. Sabina had lied to her.

'I do wish she had confided in me.' Frau Bruck twisted her wedding-ring round. She had bony, thin fingers and always did everything quickly. 'Who knows? She probably didn't want to leave. It's awful to think that she may have been forced to go against her will. You would confide in me if you had any problems like that, wouldn't you, Hannah?'

5

Berlin, May 1989

The ground shook as if there was an earthquake but people were cheering. The sun shone and little children stretched forwards waving their black and red and gold paper flags with the tiny hammer and compasses in the centre. Hannah caught sight of a little girl with curly blonde hair sitting on her father's shoulder, cheering and laughing and waving her flag, and she thought of the photo they still had on one of the bookshelves in their living-room. Hannah, aged four, sitting on her father's shoulders waving a black, red and gold striped paper flag with the sign of the hammer and compasses in the middle. The girl in the photo looked so happy, her blue eyes reflecting the clear blue sky, and her father looked so young and handsome. Hannah's mother had taken the photo. That was why her father wanted to keep it.

Hannah supposed she must have felt happy on the day the photograph was taken, just like all the children she saw around her, bouncing up and down, waving and shouting as each new tank rumbled past and made the pavements rock. The children blew kisses at the soldiers, while their mothers and grandmothers shrieked, 'Blow them a kiss! Show the young men how you can blow a kiss!' But the soldiers only had eyes for the platform where the Party leaders stood. Stern soldier's eyes all turned at the same angle to the left, towards the old men in their grey coats and trilby hats and mud-grey generals' uniforms.

But perhaps it was only the photograph of the little girl with short, blonde, curly hair and tiny pearls of teeth that made Hannah think she had ever been happy on May Day. Her mother had always loved that photograph and talked proudly about the things Hannah had done that day. One Russian soldier, who had been watching the parade, had talked to her father in Russian, telling him how beautiful Hannah was, how she reminded him of his little sister at home. He picked her up so that Hannah's mother could take a photo of them both together, but Hannah had been scared of the strange man with his strange language and had knocked his hat off so that it scooted across the pavement. Mama and Papa used to laugh when they told how the Russian soldier had carefully put Hannah down and then picked up his machine-gun and pretended to take aim, first at Hannah, then at Mama and Papa and then back at Hannah. But when they told the story once in front of Oma, she was shocked. 'If you'd seen what the Russians did after the war,' she said, 'you wouldn't laugh at a thing like that.'

Hannah remembered other times they had been to the May Day parade, years and years where they had all been to the great parade together, all waving their paper flags and afterwards having a picnic in the park with Sabina's family. Every year, they talked about the other parades they'd seen and argued about which one was the best. And Sabina's father talked excitedly about the new weapons and tanks they had seen while everyone else told him he was boring. He was a doctor, but he knew everything there was to know about tanks.

Then, about three years ago, Hannah's mother started to dislike the parade. First, she said that it was boring and that it was a sham because people weren't really happy to be there. Hannah couldn't understand her. She and Sabina had a wonderful time, cheering and waving their flags and dancing in time to the military bands; if you could call it dancing when there were so many people it was almost impossible to move. And they got lots of sweets to eat afterwards. Later, Hannah's mother started to say she didn't want to go to the parade because there were too many tanks and guns, and she thought East Germany was meant to be against militarism.

'If we're for peace, why do they spend so much money on weapons?' she used to say. And Hannah's father said, 'Come on. You're taking it all too seriously. It's only a parade. People like a bit of a show.' They hadn't had a picnic with Sabina's family for a long time. Then last year, Hannah's mother had decided she just wouldn't go to the parade at all. Everyone was supposed to go. You had to turn up at the meeting place where your school or firm was assembled and let them check your name off a list. Papa wanted Mama to do at least that, at least get her name checked off. But she said that was worse than not going at all, pretending you were there and then going home again. So she didn't go, and nothing bad happened to her at work.

The tanks rumbled past and people cheered and Hannah didn't know what she was doing there. This year, it was her father who had refused to attend the May Day parade. When Hannah asked him if he would go with her, he sighed and said, 'No'. He was sitting on the old sofa with a newspaper in his hand, but Hannah knew he wasn't reading the newspaper; he was just using it so he wouldn't have to talk to her.

Hannah waited at the door which led straight from their living-room into the corridor outside the flat. She wished she could remind him of all the things he had said to Mama the year before. She was worried about him. Perhaps he would lose his job. He at least ought to show his face, get his name checked off on the list, so he wouldn't get into any trouble at work. But she didn't say anything. She just stood there watching him, and after a while her father said, 'Hannah, how can I go?'

Hannah didn't know what she was doing at the parade. She had stayed so long with her father, waiting to see if he would change his mind, that she had had to run all the way to the Pioneer Palace, knowing she would get shouted at because her tie had worked loose and she had forgotten to clean her boots. They didn't like her wearing her ankle boots with her Pioneer uniform.

Children dressed up in Pioneer uniforms were jumping around all over the steps of the building, mixed up with parents trying to take photographs of the younger ones. A small boy pointed at Hannah. 'Look, Mama! That girl's wearing jeans.' But Hannah didn't care. She knew she wasn't the only one. Group leaders were standing at the top of the steps with letters held high on a card. Hannah couldn't even remember what letter her group was supposed to have. She hadn't been listening at the last meeting.

She liked going along to the Pioneer Palace for drawing and painting classes, but the meetings where they talked about parades, or where they sat around the photo of Erich Honecker and talked about writing him a letter for his birthday, were really boring. It was only Sabina who ever really listened to what they said. And when Hannah had decided once that she would stop going to Pioneers and only go to the painting classes, it was Sabina who had persuaded her to stay. 'You'll do better at school if you keep going to Pioneers,' she said. 'My Papa says so.'

But now Sabina was gone. At her very first Pioneer meeting without Sabina, Hannah had spent the whole time staring at a painting Sabina had done, years ago, when they were both in kindergarten. It was just before they started school. Everyone in their kindergarten group had had to paint a picture with the title, 'Daddy is a soldier'. Sabina's father had never been a soldier. Hannah never found out why. But even though her father had never been in the army, Sabina's painting had won first prize and hung on the wall of their Pioneer group's room ever since. They had even made a painting book called, 'Daddy is a soldier', with a blank page next to each of the winning paintings from every Pioneer group in Berlin—so other children could copy them.

Hannah was surprised that Sabina's painting was still on the wall now that her family had gone away. A man in a muddy, green uniform, but with a big smile on his brick-red face stood next to a muddy, green tank. The picture was under glass and had a red frame, but the card with Sabina's name on it had grown yellow and curled up at the edges, so that it would soon fall off the wall all by itself. Hannah had stared at the picture for so long, she hadn't noticed anything they said at the meeting. Presumably the picture had hung on the wall for so many years that nobody noticed it was there any longer. At school, Sabina's pictures had been removed from the classroom wall before Hannah arrived back on the first day, and her name had been painted out of the awards board for good students in the Socialist State.

Hannah walked rapidly up and down in front of the Pioneers' building, scanning the crowd for someone she knew. One of her group was bound to call out to her as soon as they saw her. Paul Sehr had even phoned up the night before and asked if he should call for her, but Hannah didn't want that. There were so many children running around, some pursued by mothers anxious to arrange and then rearrange their hair or their Pioneer ties, that it took Hannah more than ten minutes to realize that the older groups must already have moved off to join on to the big parade. 'Excuse me.' She interrupted a mother who was trying to smooth down the hair of her twin boys both at the same time. The woman had a plastic bottle full of water with her, which she poured into her hand and then rubbed into their short, stubbly hair before attempting to smooth it down. Both boys were impatient and kept turning round, so that their hair stood on end even more after each attempt to straighten it out. The mother was red in the face and angry. 'Papa will be ashamed of you!' She whirled round to look at Hannah. 'What do you want?'

'Excuse me. You haven't seen any big kids—from the seventh or eighth class—have you?' The woman grabbed hold of one of the twins, whose Pioneer tie had come loose and was about to drop on the floor, 'My God! You're really late! I wouldn't like to be in your shoes! They left about ten minutes ago.'

'My father's not well and I had to give him his medicine before I could get away,' Hannah lied. She was angry with herself for the lie and set off again, running in the direction she knew her group would have gone. There were always big hold-ups along the parade route. She was bound to catch up with them.

But after running to the next street corner, Hannah stopped and walked. She didn't want to catch up with her group after all. There would be trouble whatever she did and she didn't want to lie any more. She decided she would go home and then simply turn up at school the next day and tell the truth: she hadn't really wanted to come to the parade; she hadn't set off until the last minute and she had arrived too late. She told herself she didn't care what they did to her. Then she remembered that her father would worry about her if she turned up at home before the parade was over, so instead of going home she kept on walking in the direction of Unter den Linden, the main street the parade would pass.

She ripped off her Pioneer tie and stuffed it into the pocket of her jeans. Then, even though she felt hot, she put on her red anorak to cover up her Pioneer blouse. Perhaps people would think she was a tourist from the West. The thin, red nylon anorak was another present from Sabina's uncle from West Berlin. Hannah had an uncle in the West as well, but he never wanted to send them presents. He said that they ought to go and live in West Germany if they wanted the kind of clothes people wore in the West.

There would be no more presents from the West now. Not unless Sabina sent her something. But Sabina had been away for two weeks and Hannah still had no idea where she was. She had assumed Frau Bruck was telling the truth when she said she didn't know whether Sabina's family had left through Hungary or Czechoslovakia. But you could never be sure anyone was telling the truth. Perhaps Sabina's parents had been arrested and she and her sister had been put in a children's home. Perhaps they had never even made it to the West.

And then again, if Sabina and her family were really in the West, letters from them probably wouldn't get through. Hannah's father had already told her the Stasi would be checking all his letters and phone calls after they shot her mother. When Hannah asked him how long they'd be doing that for, he just shrugged his shoulders.

Near the Opera House on Unter den Linden, Hannah was finally able to squeeze through the crowd and get herself a place almost next to the street. Some teenagers from other parts of East Germany had posters on sticks, and banners which they carried stretched out between two of them so they could tag on to the end of the parade and march through the streets with people cheering at them. You could tell they came from the country. Their posters weren't very original. One of the banners read, '*Ich bin dabei*—I belong.' Hannah didn't feel as if she belonged.

She didn't belong anywhere any more. There was no way she could belong in a country where they shot her mother and then told lies about it. But she had seen and heard about what it was like in the West and she was sure she wouldn't belong there either. In the West there were hundreds of people with no homes who had to sleep under bridges out on the streets, whatever the weather. And when they did find a warm place, in the underground stations or huddled up over a warm air shaft, the police came along and moved them on. At least, in East Germany no one had to sleep out on the streets. In the West there were millions of people who had no work. They had learned about that at school; millions and millions of people who had no jobs and got so little money that they ended up sleeping out on the streets. Even in cities like London in England where there were hundreds and thousands of rich people, they had poor people sleeping out on the pavements. Hannah knew she didn't belong in a world like that, where rich people walked past poor people sleeping on the pavements and just ignored them. In the DDR, everyone had a job. Everyone had enough to eat. Everyone had somewhere to live, even if their flats were very small. At least they weren't sleeping on the streets. Hannah stared at the group of teenagers just beside her, waving their posters and cheering and shouting, 'Long live Erich Honecker', and wished she could feel she belonged, just as much as they did.

Surely, Hannah thought, her mother had been wrong, wanting to go to the West, where they were cruel and let people sleep on the streets. She knew that her mother wasn't the sort of person who was only interested in what you could buy in the West, the things they saw in the advertisements when they watched West TV. It wasn't the stupid cooker that had made her mother get so desperate she had tried to drive through a checkpoint to the West, or the fact that they had only just got a car after waiting for one since the year Hannah was born. It was something that had happened at her mother's school. Whatever had happened at the school had convinced Hannah's mother that she didn't belong any more. Hannah was sure her father must know what had happened. But he never mentioned her mother and she didn't want to upset him by asking. They hardly talked to each other any more.

Perhaps her mother had made a mistake about what happened at her school. She could have been over-reacting. And perhaps the way her mother died had been an accident. What if they hadn't really meant to shoot her? Hannah supposed that they would keep quiet about it, tell lies just so no one would hear what had really happened. If her mother's death had been an accident, Hannah could learn to belong again.

'Naughty! Well, I never would have expected to find you bunking off. Hallo! Your name's Gretel, or something like that, isn't it?'

Hannah didn't recognize the girl in the black leather jacket with fringes on it. She was a very pretty girl, with dark brown curly hair and huge brown eyes, the sort of girl all the boys were interested in. Not that Hannah wanted boys to be interested in her.

Hannah thought she had seen the girl somewhere before, but she couldn't think where.

'Hey! Don't panic. I won't tell. What d'you think I'm doing here?' The girl squeezed right up to the barrier, beside Hannah, forcing a boy from the banner-waving group to move back a step. He looked very annoyed and brushed away at the sleeve of his Pioneer shirt as if the girl had thrown sand

50

at him. 'Sorry.' The girl grinned and then stuck out her tongue at him. 'I didn't know this pavement was private property.' Then she leaned forward over the crowd-control barrier and chanted, 'We love you, Gorbi! Gorbachev for President.'

Hannah blushed. Everyone was looking in their direction. All around them people were laughing, while the teenagers from the country looked very shocked and started to wave their banners again and their flags in black, red and gold. 'Long live Erich Honecker,' they shouted. The girl laughed at them and had to shout back even louder as another tank brigade rolled past. 'He can live as long as he likes. There's an old people's home just down the road where he can live happily ever after. But we need a leader who'll do something. Gorbi! Gorbi!'

Hannah smiled, but she looked all round to see who else was listening. She had never heard anyone talking like that girl before. She knew there were lots of people who thought like her, but none of them ever said what they thought. She knew at once that her father would have warned her to keep away from someone like that. 'She'll only make trouble for you,' Papa would have said. But Hannah didn't care. She spoke to the girl under cover of the chanting which their neighbours had started up again. 'Two, four, six, eight, who do we appreciate? Erich! Erich!'

'Do you always talk like that?' Hannah asked.

'You should know what I'm like,' the girl said. Then she pursed her lips together hard and wrinkled up her nose in a pantomime of anger. 'I've only been in your class for four days.'

'Oh.' Hannah's eyes opened wide. She had avoided the new girl all week. She couldn't even remember her name. 'What happened to your hair?'

The new girl ran her hands through her brown curls. 'Good, eh? This is my own. Honest. But I can't remember what I had on last week at school. It was a wig. My mum works drawing pictures for children's books and we've got all

51

kinds of props at home. She used to get me to dress up sometimes and then she drew me, when I was little. Gorbi! Gorbi!' She grinned again at the oldest boy in the group squashed up next to them in the crowd. 'Got to keep them on their toes!' she whispered to Hannah.

'You had tomato-red hair at school,' said Hannah. 'It looked horrible.'

'Yeh,' said the girl, 'I wanted to make a good impression in my first week.'

Hannah remembered that the girl's last name was Ahmed, but she still couldn't remember her first name.

'Does your dad come from Arabia?' she asked.

'What?'

A troop of soldiers marched past, drumming their metal-capped boots on the tarmac, red faces glowing in the sun as they concentrated on staying in step.

'Does your dad come from Arabia?' Hannah shouted.

'There's no such place, Gretel. Tut, tut. They don't teach you much geography at our school, do they?'

'My name's not Gretel.'

'All right, then, Gretchen, Gunilla, Griselda Gorbi! Gorbi!'

'My name's Hannah.'

The girl suddenly looked over Hannah's shoulder and Hannah turned to look behind her. The crowd was slowly parting and two men in leather jackets, both carrying neat shoulder-bags, were ploughing their way towards them. The group of teenagers from the country were smiling now, smiling at them like foxes who've found their way in to a henhouse.

'*Dummkopf!*' the girl whispered. 'Whatever you do, don't ever tell anyone your real name. You've forgotten your pass, right?' She ducked down and suddenly slithered under the crash barrier. Hannah watched her sprinting for twenty or thirty metres through the safest part of the parade—in amongst the marching soldiers who weren't allowed to look anywhere except straight ahead, and then lost her as she slipped underneath a barrier further along the street and was gone.

The two men crashed through the crowd and stood over Hannah and the other young people around her.

'Right! Which one's the troublemaker? Do we have to arrest the whole lot of you, or are you going to tell us who was shouting slogans against the State?'

The group of teenagers from the country looked scared stiff. The grown-ups who had been standing around smiling while the girl chanted her slogans for Gorbachev slowly disappeared.

'She's gone,' said Hannah. 'She went under the barrier when she saw you coming.'

Hannah thought the officer with the notebook looked more like a farmer than a man from the Stasi. He had rosy red cheeks and white-blond hair. 'All right. Give us her name.'

'I don't know her name,' said Hannah. 'Any of you lot know her name?' The endless parade of soldiers and tanks, trucks and motorbikes was nearly coming to an end and in the distance Hannah could see the rows of blue neckties of the Young Pioneer Brigades from all over Berlin.

'I thought you knew her.' The boy who had lost his place near the barrier must have had hay fever or a cold because he kept sneezing. Hannah shook her head. 'Never seen her in my life before,' she said. 'She had a cheek, didn't she, shoving you out of the way like that.'

The boy sneezed. 'But she said your name. I heard her. Gretchen or Gretel or something.'

'She was just saying any old names.' Hannah was getting very hot in her red anorak. 'My name's not Gretel. Nothing like it.'

'Well, you may as well tell us your real name.' The other man from the Stasi made Hannah feel sick and scared. He had the same white, puffy bulldog face as the man who had been there in the high-walled, white-tiled room with her mother. Strange, how she had never noticed until now how many men from the police looked like that. 'It's Sabina.

Sabina Schott.' For a moment, Hannah thought about telling them she had come over from West Berlin for the day, but then she would have to show a West German pass.

'I've forgotten my pass,' she said. 'My dad's sick you see, and he felt really bad just before I had to come out to the parade and I forgot my pass.' The lie was getting better. Hannah could tell that they believed her, that she was going to get away with it this time. She showed how upset she was. Her voice lowered so that the Pioneer group from the country all leaned over to hear what she was saying. 'And then, when I got to the Pioneer Palace, my group had already set off. The whole day's been a disaster. And then that strange girl came along.'

The younger Stasi man finished writing down the name she had given him and Sabina's old address, which she also knew off by heart. 'Well, we'd better move on,' he said. 'Enjoy yourselves.'

Hannah had to get away. She pushed back through the crowd and started on the long walk home. The streets to the side of Unter den Linden were almost empty, but she couldn't get rid of the feeling that someone was following her, someone who would find out her real name and tell the Stasi she was lying.

They had gone camping near the North Sea once, when Hannah was eight, and she and her mother had set off to walk as far as they could along the coast. Soon after they had left the campsite, the beach became less sandy and was strewn with huge boulders that were warmed by the sun. Hannah loved the feel of the warm, smooth rocks under her bare feet and wanted to walk on further and further. She felt safe and warm and happy, far away from Berlin.

Then suddenly a snake had whip-lashed out of a crack in a rock, snip snap, whipping around back and forth away from her mother's bare feet, her mother doing a wild dance to escape the snake and the snake curling and twisting desperately until it shot off into the brush. Afterwards, when they told Papa about the snake, he said it was poisonous. 'You both might have been bitten. You might have died.' The lies Hannah told made her feel safe for a time. But they didn't disappear; they hid themselves like the snake in its crack in the warm rock, waiting to trap her, ready to wind themselves around her and inject her with their venom. There was no safe place. She had to be on her guard all the time.

6

Berlin, May 1989

The girl Hannah had seen at the May Day parade groaned and clapped her hand up to her forehead. 'You really want to know my name? My real name?'

Hannah nodded. She felt relieved when she saw the girl sauntering into the playground the day after the parade. She didn't see why she should care, but the whole evening she had sat at home pretending to read and wondering whether the girl had managed to get away completely, or whether someone had caught her and handed her over to the police.

'Well,' the girl sighed, 'in my pass it says Stefanie Iris Ahmed, but my real name is Steffi.' She looked up at the sky, blew out her cheeks and whistled. Her hair, which had cascaded in wild curls the day before, was tied back neatly into a red bow. Suddenly, she stopped whistling. 'You were a real idiot yesterday,' she said, 'shouting your name out like that, in front of all those Simple Simons from the country. That sort'd sell their own grandmother to the Stasi.'

Hannah was mad, 'You call me stupid? I wasn't the one who shouted out slogans for Gorbachev when we were supposed to be shouting for Honecker. I wasn't the one who slipped out right into the path of the parade. You could have been killed by one of those dirty great tanks!'

Steffi shrugged her shoulders. 'See if I care. Anyway, there weren't any tanks, only soldiers. And they're not allowed to stop marching, whatever comes in front of them. All part of them learning to be disciplined.'

'But you nearly got me into trouble, too.'

'Yeh. I was worried about that. Honest.'

'They all thought I knew you.'

Steffi grinned. 'I thought you'd be clever enough to get out

56

of that one. That's why I didn't tell you my name. So's you wouldn't have to tell a lie.'

Hannah didn't say anything. She had got so used to telling lies that she hardly even noticed any longer whether she was lying or telling the truth.

Hannah couldn't talk to Steffi during the lessons. Frau Bruck had given her Sabina's place, at the far side of the classroom. But they sat next to each other at lunchtime.

'They can't do much wrong with potato soup.' Steffi sat down at the long wooden table and shook salt over her bowl. Then she lifted her spoon, blowing hard on the steaming hot liquid. At the other side of the table, Paul Sehr watched her over his spoon as he shovelled soup and bread into his mouth, hardly stopping long enough to breathe. Steffi blew once more on her spoon, wrinkled up her nose and then moved the spoon carefully away from her face so she could examine it.

'Yeuck!' she said. 'That's not even potato. It's lumps of thick, white fat.' Hannah looked into her own bowl of soup and her stomach churned. She hadn't started eating and she put down her spoon. Paul Sehr, who had finished his lunch, looked anxiously at them both for a second and then pulled both bowls over to his side of the table. He was pale and bony and looked as if there was something eating away at him inside so fast that he never, ever got enough to eat.

'We ought to get up a petition for better school meals.' Steffi took an apple out of her pocket and started eating that. For once, Paul Sehr stopped eating.

'Petitions aren't actually allowed,' he said. 'I mean, it has to be done democratically. So you have to ask me to go to the Director and talk to her about it. Because I've been democratically elected as Pioneer Secretary.' Steffi got up and walked out.

It was hot outside in the playground and Hannah found Steffi lying under the big lime tree on the grass, her black leather jacket as a pillow under her head. 'I wish I could leave this stupid place.' She was staring up at the bright, yellow-green flowers and didn't turn to look at Hannah.

57

'Lots of people feel like that,' said Hannah. 'My best friend, Sabina, left with her family a few weeks ago. I don't suppose I'll ever hear from her again.' She didn't say anything about what they had done to her mother. She didn't know Steffi well enough to talk about that.

'I could leave tomorrow if I wanted to,' said Steffi. 'I could walk out of here any time.'

'What are you on about?' Hannah sat down on the grass with her back leaning against the huge trunk of the old tree. 'You just said you wished you could go. And now you're saying you can go if you want to. Nobody can just walk out of here.'

People were only allowed to go to the West for very special occasions. Hannah's mother had once been allowed to go to West Berlin for a day, because an old aunt of hers was eighty. But she hardly knew Hannah's great-aunt. She had had to apply to go to the birthday party a year in advance, and she was only given permission as long as Hannah and her father didn't go—so she would have a good reason to come back. 'You'll have to apply months in advance if you want to go to the West,' Hannah said. 'And even then, they'll only let you stay for a day.'

'Not me,' said Steffi. 'I've got an Algerian passport, because of my dad. I can leave any time I want.'

'Why don't you then?'

'Why should I? I live here. My mum lives here. My cats live here. I just get fed up with the way they treat everyone like children. They treat my mum like a child and she's thirty-nine.'

'Does your dad ever take you to Algeria? You could have a good holiday there.'

'He hasn't got any money.' Steffi sat up, pulled the red ribbon out of her hair and then lay down on the grass again. 'I haven't seen my dad for a while, anyway. He lives in West Berlin.'

'But why didn't you and your mum go with him?'

'Why should we? I told you. We live here. Max and Moritz live here. This is our country. I don't want to be a Westi.'

58

'Don't you miss him?' Hannah never told anyone how much she missed her mother, not even her father.

'He's happier over there in the West.' Steffi sat up and slowly started to tug her curls back and smooth them into a pony-tail. 'My mum says that when he first got here from Algeria, he couldn't speak a word of German and he didn't know a thing about Germany. He didn't know that there were two Germanys. He thought it was all one, big rich country. They promised him he could train to be a doctor, but when he got married and decided to stay here, they made him stop his training because they didn't want foreign doctors. All he could do was be a taxi driver. He was the best taxi driver in East Berlin.' Steffi yanked two ends of her long, curly hair to tighten up her pony-tail. 'But then he moved to West Berlin, so he could carry on with his training.'

'Is he a doctor now?'

'Nah.' Steffi stood up and brushed grass off the back of her skirt. 'They don't let foreigners get proper jobs as doctors over there either. He's working as a hospital porter. As far as I know.'

'The Whit Festival is going to be even more fun than usual.' Paul Sehr sat next to Frau Bruck in the circle. He looked down at his shirt while he was speaking and smoothed the ends of his red tie flat on to his shirt.

'Why does he always wear his Pioneer uniform?' Steffi nudged Hannah. Paul was the only one in the class who had a red Pioneer tie instead of a blue one, because he had once been chosen to take part in a special Pioneer camp.

'He's really proud of it. His mother's something big in the Party. But his dad went over to West Berlin.'

Steffi giggled and lifted up her pony-tail from behind, twisting it round to make a knot on the top of her head. It was so boring, listening to Paul talking about the Whit Festival. Even maths was better.

'Oh. There's someone over there volunteering. I think

Stefanie would like to go to the Festival, Paul.' Frau Bruck smiled at her.

'Oh, no! I can't.' Steffi pulled her hands down out of her hair and held them tightly in her lap. 'My cats ae both sick,' she said. 'And you know how long you have to wait at the vet's.'

'But the Festival is on Sunday,' said Paul. 'You'll probably be able to leave your cats by then.'

Steffi glared at him. 'My cats are really, really ill,' she said.

Nobody wanted to go.

'You should try in Class 8,' Steffi said. 'They're the ones who should be going. They're in the FDJ already. The Whit Festival is for them, for the Youth Party, not for Pioneers.'

'But this is a fantastic opportunity to show our support and our enthusiasm as young socialists.' Paul's thin face was red and sweaty, and the minute he caught Steffi's eye he closed his own eyes or stared at the floor. 'It's not often that Pioneers get the chance to go to FDJ discos and pop concerts. It's only because it's the 40th anniversary of the DDR. I mean, we really ought to do something to celebrate that.' The rest of the class stared at Paul and he shuffled his polished black shoes along the polished green floor.

'Anyone can hear the pop concert!' said Steffi. 'You can hear it all over the Alex. We don't have to go to your boring political meetings just to hear the concerts.'

Hannah saw Frau Bruck writing something down in the class record book and knew she was writing about Steffi. But Steffi must know that, too. Hannah couldn't understand why she should want to say things like that—things that would get her reported to the Director.

They didn't have Saturday school that weekend because Berlin was filled with teenagers in Pioneer uniforms and older kids from the FDJ. Hannah longed to get away, right away from teenagers pretending to have a good time because they had all been paid to travel to Berlin and look as if they were having a good time.

She could have stayed at home to avoid the crowds, but at

home she had to talk to Papa. Hannah never knew what to say to him any more. They spent most of their time not talking about her mother; trying so hard not to upset each other that there was nothing more to say. Every day, Papa looked at Hannah anxiously and asked her how she was feeling. And every day she said 'Oh, I'm fine.' Or sometimes she snapped at him, 'How do you think I am? There's nothing wrong with me, is there?' She couldn't stand being alone with him and she knew that he was relieved too, when she went away.

So she arranged to meet Steffi on the Alex even though they both knew it would be impossible to move in the city, with thousands of members of the FDJ wandering around not knowing what they were there for. You could always tell the ones who came from the country. They were the ones who really looked as if they were enjoying themselves, because it was the first time some of them had ever been to East Berlin. They gasped in amazement at the things in shop windows and rushed around with carrier bags from the Central Department Store.

'They haven't got a clue,' Steffi said. She bought them both an ice-cream and they sat down at the top of the long flight of steps under the TV Tower. 'Yeuck! There's a slug.'

Hannah looked down at the steps, but Steffi was looking straight ahead, at a young man with short cropped hair.

'Can I sit here?' he said.

Steffi shrank away. 'I'm allergic to slugs,' she groaned. Hannah moved further along the step and Steffi moved up close to her, pushing her again.

'Be like that. If you didn't have an ice-cream already, I'd buy you each one to celebrate.'

Steffi made a face as if she had tasted poison. 'I don't eat slug ice-cream.' Hannah nudged her. Steffi was going too far.

'What have you got to celebrate?'

'You must have heard about it, on West TV.' Steffi sat up straight and made a face as if she'd just eaten a lemon. No one was really supposed to watch West TV.

'You Stasis must think we're really dumb,' she said. 'Of

course we don't watch West TV. I wouldn't know how to, would you, Griselda?' Hannah grinned and shook her head.

'Well, it's coming on our TV tonight.'

Steffi pretended not to listen, puffing her cheeks out and whistling quietly.

'They're making the army smaller—even before the West has agreed to make their armies smaller.'

Steffi stopped whistling. 'What's that got to do with us?'

'It's got a lot to do with me,' the young man said. 'I've just finished my time in the army and now I know they'll never call me up again. Anyway, you look different to the others. You look like the sort who would be interested in the peace movement.'

'Are you nuts?' Steffi jumped up and walked away in the direction of the big red church.

'You didn't have to be like that to him.' Hannah ran after her. 'He was really happy about finishing the army. It wasn't his fault that he had to be in it. Everyone has to—if they want to get anywhere. Like the FDJ. Nobody really wants to join, except Paul Sehr. But they have to. Otherwise, they won't stand a chance of getting a job. You can't blame him. He wouldn't have got a job if he hadn't joined up.'

'And if everyone didn't join the army?' said Steffi. 'Then they wouldn't have anyone to do all their rotten jobs.' She smiled. 'Just imagine what would happen if there was a war and all the soldiers decided not to turn up and fight.'

She pushed past Hannah, strode towards the Alexander-platz and was lost in the crowd. By the time Hannah got to the railway bridge, she was ready to give up looking for Steffi and go home. But suddenly Steffi ran back towards her. 'Come and look at this. Come on!' She grabbed hold of Hannah's hand and pulled her towards the fountain at the centre of the square. Cameras from East German television were trained on a group of teenagers in their FDJ uniforms, linking arms and singing a patriotic song. Paul Sehr's Pioneer uniform stood out in the crowd and the TV interviewer made for him.

'Are you enjoying yourself?'

'Oh, yes.' Paul's face turned red and his thin, blond hair was wet from the sweat on his glistening forehead. 'I mean, this is what it's all about, isn't it? I feel really honoured that my class chose me to be here.'

'Rubbish!' Steffi was so loud that all the people around them started to laugh. 'They had to pay him to come. No one would come to one of these things unless they paid them.'

The interviewer rounded off his programme. 'The Whit Festival is proof, if anyone still needed proof, that our young people in the socialist part of Germany really do know how to enjoy themselves.' The group around the fountain all cheered as he finished speaking and stopped cheering just as the theme music faded away and the producer dropped his arm.

As the group moved away from the fountain, Steffi pushed past them clutching her throat. 'Out of the way. Out of the way,' she said. 'I think I'm going to be sick.'

Steffi wasn't sick. She laughed when everyone had gone away, but Hannah shouted at her. 'You shouldn't pretend like that. Some of them were really scared you were going to make a mess of their uniforms.' Then she laughed out loud.

'They deserve it,' Steffi giggled. 'And anyway, it's enough to make anyone sick. They all get paid for coming here and cheering and looking as if they're enjoying themselves. And people sitting in their armchairs watching TV tonight will think it's all true.'

'They can always watch West TV.'

'Not in Dresden they can't. My uncle calls Dresden the Valley of the Clueless because they can't get West TV. Nobody in Dresden has any idea what's going on in the rest of the world.'

Steffi had noticed someone. 'She looks like a good bet,' she said to Hannah. Like a powerful zoom lense, her eyes picked people out in crowds and let her track them until she had them within talking distance. Then she closed in. 'Are you from America?'

The woman in the floppy beige sunhat and black sunglasses smiled. She spoke German with a very strong

American accent, but she didn't make any mistakes when she spoke. 'Well, goodness. How did you know that?'

Steffi twisted her hands behind her back and shrugged her shoulders like a little girl who is rather sweet and shy. Hannah watched her, fascinated, wondering what her next trick was going to be. 'I suppose I could sort of tell that you don't come from Berlin,' Steffi said.

The woman told them that her grandfather was from Germany, from Leipzig. Then she explained that she taught German at a college in Illinois. 'It's not as bad here as people back in the States say it is,' she said. 'I've taken some wonderful photos and your policemen are so helpful if you know what to say to them. All I need now, is to buy some books. Do you know a good bookshop round here?'

Steffi smiled sweetly. 'Yes,' she said. 'You're right about the policemen being helpful if you say the right words to them. Things have improved a little. I mean, there's only been one other shooting incident since they shot Hannah's mother. And that was nearly six weeks ago.'

Hannah froze. Pain shot through her shoulders and her eyes and throat stung. She hadn't told Steffi about her mother. The others in the class must have told her. But it was her life, not Steffi's. Steffi had no right to tell this strange American woman about her. The woman lifted up her black sunglasses and stared at Hannah.

'Oh, my God! That is bad!' Her eyes were a sort of washed-out blue. Hannah had the impression she would have made the same comment if Steffi had told her they had just lost an umbrella. 'Tell me all about it,' she said.

Hannah was quiet. She thought of the woman telling her friends back home in Illinois how she'd seen the Berlin Wall, the TV Tower and the girl whose mother got herself shot. For a second, she thought of walking away, leaving Steffi to enjoy her little game of entertaining the American tourist, but then she stayed. Her fear of being taken away from her father and put in a children's home was a length of rope around her neck that started to tighten whenever she wanted to tell the truth or show her true feelings. If Steffi saw that she was upset, she might tell someone else in the class, someone who would definitely tell Frau Bruck. Hannah had no way of knowing if she could trust Frau Bruck and she knew even less about Steffi. She had to keep up the lie, to tell the story that Steffi must have heard already from the others.

'I don't know much,' she said. 'We hadn't seen her for six months before it happened. So I didn't feel all that bad. I'll show you where the bookshop is, if you like.'

They took the American woman to the House of Good Books. Steffi grinned when the woman complained about having to queue up before they went in. 'Oh, we get used to that,' she said. 'It's because they haven't got enough shopping baskets and you have to have one of their shopping baskets before they let you in.' After the woman had found the books she wanted, Hannah took her upstairs. They had to walk through the children's book section to find Steffi, thumbing through the records.

'Wouldn't you like to choose yourselves a book?' the woman said. 'I ought to give you something. You've been so kind to me.' Hannah had looked through the teenage section the week before and one glance told her there was nothing new. All the books for teenagers were boring stories to do with the Whit Festival and there was a pile of diaries for teenagers who were just about to join the FDJ.

'Yeuck!' Steffi picked up a diary and put it down again, rubbing her hands together as if she had found a slug sticking to one of the books. Hannah looked round to see who was listening to them. Steffi was always so loud.

'Hm. This would be great to show my students in the States.' The American woman picked up one of the diaries. An assistant rushed to take it out of her hands.

'Don't touch unless you are going to buy.'

'But I am going to buy.' The American woman tried to snatch the book back and took off her sunglasses so she could get a good look at the assistant. 'Can I see the manager, please?'

Steffi took her arm and led her away. 'Leave it,' she said, whispering now. 'They won't let you buy an FDJ diary. There aren't enough copies. They don't let anyone buy them except for the idiots who join up.'

'Well, won't you two be needing one?' the woman insisted. 'Don't you have to join that thing when you're about fourteen?'

'We don't have to,' said Steffi. She turned and walked back to the records.

'We do really,' whispered Hannah, 'if we want to do well at school and everything. Steffi's just angry about it. She's bound to join as well.' She picked up a diary. 'I have to join in about two weeks. There's this big party we have and then we become real members of the Socialist State.'

'Oh, do tell me about it.' The woman put her sunglasses back on and put Hannah's diary in her basket. 'If I'm not mistaken, there's a nice little hotel where you can buy very good cakes round here. Let me buy you both something to eat before you go home and you can tell me all about your party for the FDJ.'

The Palace Hotel was one of the biggest in Berlin. The place with the best cakes was the part where you couldn't pay with East German marks. 'No problem,' the woman said. 'I have dollars. Sit down and tell me about this party you're going to have.'

'It's called the *Jugendweihe*,' Hannah said. 'It's a kind of initiation ceremony.'

Steffi stood up, took hold of her chair and shoved it back under the table. 'Hannah, you're not going through with all that! You never told me! After what they did to your mother?'

Hannah was glad that Steffi had had the good sense to whisper. Except that her agitated whispers seem to have attracted more attention than her usual way of talking. 'Sit down. I haven't had the chance to tell you. I've only known you for a week. And anyway, everyone in our class is going through with the *Jugendweihe*. You're treated more like an

66

adult,' she explained. The woman was writing everything down in a black notebook with a red spine.

Steffi sat down again. 'Are you a spy?' She took the woman's sunhat from the table and put it in front of her eyes.

'No,' the woman laughed, 'this is my journal.'

'Are you a journalist?'

'No. It's just my journal. I just write down what's happened.'

'And are you writing down that I think Hannah is a crooked snake, joining the FDJ?' Steffi put the woman's sunglasses on.

The American woman closed her book. 'Of course not. She's only joining because you have to. You can't go to university if you don't join, can you? And it's harder to get a job, isn't it?'

'So?' Steffi sat back in the large, basket-weave armchair. 'It's better to miss university than to tell lies.' She glared at Hannah and then leaned forward to finish off her strawberry cake. 'I think I'll have to go now,' she said. 'Thanks for the cake.'

Hannah couldn't finish her cake. She wasn't hungry. Ever since Steffi had told the American woman about her mother, she had wanted to leave the two of them together and run away. She stood up as soon as Steffi had left the room. 'I have to go too,' she said.

She caught up with Steffi at the bottom of the stairs, where she was looking in the large, plate-glass windows at the dresses draped on fashion models, the prices marked in West German marks on a small card at the front of the window.

Hannah stood next to Steffi and pressed her face against the glass so that it steamed up with her breath.

'You called me a liar for deciding to join the FDJ,' she said. 'Well, I want you to know that I think you're just as much of a liar, using what happened to my mum to make friends with an American so's you can get her to buy us a cake in the Palace Hotel.'

Steffi stared at the cyclamen-coloured dress with matching

shoes. 'Nobody ever wears matching shoes here,' she said. 'You'd have to wait three years until the shoe shops had anything to match a colour like that. And then you'd still need to buy an underskirt for the dress. And that'd take you another two years. And then the dress'd be out of fashion.'

'It's even worse than lying!' Hannah whispered. 'Telling Americans hard-luck stories just so they'll treat us to cake. Like we're poor relations or something.'

'She bought you your FDJ diary, didn't she? And you didn't mind that piece of cake.' Steffi bent down to scrutinize the small writing on the price label.

'I never ate it. How could I eat it after your lies?'

'I wasn't telling lies,' said Steffi. 'It's true. They did shoot your mother. It's you that's keeping the lie going, joining the FDJ as if nothing has happened. If I were your dad, I'd feel pretty disappointed in you.'

'He couldn't care less either way,' Hannah shouted.

But it wasn't like that. She was too ashamed and too scared to admit to Steffi that her father had told her she would have to join the FDJ. Otherwise, people might think she was taking after her mother and wanting to leave the DDR. And then she might get taken away from her father. Hannah wanted to tell the truth. It ached to feel that she couldn't tell the truth to Steffi, that she had to watch out all the time for the lies she had already told, those snakes lying curled up ready to strike.

Hannah stood up straight, away from the glass window and stepped back. She noticed that Steffi's hair ribbon was almost the same colour as the dress in the window. She wanted Steffi to like her. She couldn't bear it if Steffi thought she was like all the others in their class. But her lies had made her look like them.

'All right,' she said, 'I'm only going through with the *Jugendweihe* because everybody else is doing it. And we're having a party and my uncle's coming from the West. You've got your dad in the West and you like it when you get presents from him. Well, my uncle only comes when it's something special like that. You can't blame me. And I won't get a good job if I don't go through with it and join the FDJ.' Steffi still stared at the cyclamen-coloured dress and the matching shoes on the ridiculously thin model. 'I don't believe in any of it,' Hannah said. 'But I don't want to work all my life in a factory.'

Steffi turned round. 'I don't blame you, Hannah,' she said. 'But if everyone refused to join; or if everyone marched towards the Wall together, all joining hands and saying they wanted to walk through the border, just imagine . . .'

They walked out of the hotel and down the road towards Unter den Linden. It was getting dark.

'I still blame you, Steffi,' said Hannah, shoving her hands into the pockets of her jeans. 'I'll never speak to you if you ever do that again with tourists.'

'What?'

'Making it like a circus. Entertaining them with all the bad things that happen here. You knew she would lap it up.'

'My dad used to do it all the time, in his taxi,' Steffi said. 'It's what the tourists come for. They used to give him bigger tips when he told them how bad it is over here and then drove them back to the border at night.'

'My dad says we ought to make it better,' said Hannah, 'not go on and on about how bad it is. He says we should work to change it.'

'OK. No more tourists,' said Steffi. 'But you've got to promise to tell me the truth about your mother. No more lies.' Hannah said nothing.

Papa was downstairs in front of their block of flats when Hannah got home. 'I thought you'd be at work,' Hannah said. She walked past him and pressed the button for the lift.

'It's not working.' Hannah's father walked up the eight flights of stairs behind her and opened the door to their flat.

'Don't you have to go to work?' Hannah said. Her father usually left for the theatre at five o'clock. Her watch said seven-thirty.

'Hannah, I was worried sick about you. I thought you were going to the afternoon concert and I waited and waited. I couldn't just go off to work without knowing where you were.'

Hannah shrugged her shoulders. 'There was this American woman who didn't know her way back to the border and she thought she was going to get put in prison if she didn't get to West Berlin by midnight. Steffi and me showed her the way. You don't have to worry about me, you know. I'm not a child.'

Hannah didn't know why she lied. The truth was not much different from what she said. But she had become so used to lying. She didn't look at her father as he put his jacket on. 'I'd better get off to work now,' he said.

7

Berlin, May 1989

'If it were like this all the time, I wouldn't want it to change.' The sun was hot before ten in the morning and it was still only May. The birds were singing, there were fifteen minutes to go until the bell rang for the end of break and Steffi and Hannah lay stretched out under their linden tree at the far side of the playground. No one ever came to disturb them there. The noises of the little ones playing sounded far, far away.

'Ach, the weather's all right. But the trouble with this place,' Steffi said, 'is the lies everyone tells. All the grown-ups, I mean. Any idiot can see that they can't believe everything they say about how wonderful the DDR is. But they just keep right on saying it.'

'My Papa never says anything,' said Hannah. 'All he talks about is whose turn it is to go out and get bread. Like last night. He hardly said a word. All he said was he'd been worried about me. Then he went off to work.'

'My mum was furious with me,' said Steffi. 'She thought I'd got into trouble with the police or something.'

'My dad didn't get mad,' said Hannah. 'That's what's wrong. I know he's worried about me. All the time, he's watching me to see if I'm going to do something terrible because of my mum. But he never says what he's thinking.'

'He probably doesn't want to upset you.'

'Why should I be upset? I hadn't seen her for six months before she ran off like that. It was just stupid. They said it was an accident.'

Steffi gave Hannah the withering look she usually reserved for boys who asked her to go out with them. It was the look which said she wasn't born yesterday; the look which had

71

made countless teachers send her to stand outside their classrooms when she hadn't even said a word. Then she carried on talking, as if Hannah hadn't said anything. 'It's lies that keep this place going. And the ones who decide they can't tell lies any more get thrown out.'

Hannah didn't want Steffi trying to get at the truth about her mother. She wished she could trust Steffi. But you couldn't trust anyone. She had thought she could trust Sabina until Sabina had gone off without telling her. She hadn't even written since she'd gone. There was probably something Steffi was hiding as well.

'Did your dad get thrown out because he wanted to tell the truth?'

'He's a foreigner and that's different. He just left when he wanted to. But my mum's different, too. She tells her boss when she doesn't like something. And she tells me the truth, whatever I ask her.'

Hannah's mother hadn't told her what she was planning to do. Her mother had lied when she left their house for ever. That was the hardest thing, knowing that her own mother and father had lied to her.

'There isn't a single adult in this whole country who'll tell you the truth. We know they're lying and they know they're lying. But not one of them'll even tell you they know that everyone else is lying. Except my mum and some of her friends. But they don't count. That's all at home, in private. It's what's outside that matters, what people'll tell you in public.'

Steffi closed her eyes, so that it looked for a minute as if she had fallen asleep. Then she sat up. 'I reckon if we found one grown-up who'd tell us the truth—just one—this country would be a better place.'

She looked straight at Hannah and grinned like she did whenever a teacher told her to stand outside the classroom. 'Let's do that,' she said. 'Let's go looking for people who'll tell us the truth.'

Hannah sat up and stretched out her arms over her head as

72

if she was going to swing herself up into the tree. 'We'll never get anyone to speak out. We'll never change this place.'

'We can try,' said Steffi.

It was near the end of the Citizenship lesson. The most boring lesson of the week was only ever interesting when someone played tricks on Herr Klein. But no one had been playing tricks on him lately. He was due to retire in three weeks, as soon as he'd seen his class through their Initiation and got them all joined up in the FDJ.

Herr Klein looked like a racoon, with grey-white rings around his brown eyes and two peaks of dark brown hair that stood up like extra ears above his bald head whenever he forgot to smooth them down with water in the morning. He looked like someone's battered old bear left behind on a train. He looked like a little boy, surprised by the fact that he had already grown up. He looked like a clown who'd taken his make-up off and forgotten to remove the big, sad, white circles round his eyes. When he sat in front of the class, he looked like the sort of boy every bully picks on, a boy who's just survived being grabbed by the collar and shaken until his teeth rattled. He had a stammer when he talked. Herr Klein had started out as a Latin teacher after the war, but the new DDR needed Citizenship teachers more, so he had been a Citizenship teacher at the same school for thirty-five years.

It was Steffi who first noticed that he wasn't stammering or taking twice as long as anyone else to get through a sentence. She turned round to grin at Hannah and, lifting her right hand with an imaginary glass to knock back an imaginary dose of rum, she pointed at Herr Klein. He saw her and his purple-grey face turned red, all except the large, pale rings round his eyes.

'I want you all to concentrate today. Especially you, Stefanie.'

Herr Klein's little blue and purple hands looked like paws. He folded his hands in front of him on the table and looked round the class. It was the first time Hannah had ever known them to be quiet in Herr Klein's lesson. Normally, she sat there feeling sorry for him, scared in case the Director came in and told him to leave the school at once and never come back. So many lessons had been ruined because they talked and never stopped talking while Herr Klein stammered in front of the blackboard, that Hannah had often wondered why Paul Sehr had never told on him, why nobody had ever told on Herr Klein in all the years he'd been a teacher. His was the only lesson where all the kids talked and no one worried about being reported.

But they were quiet now. 'There's something I'm worried about.' Herr Klein pushed at the ends of his short, round fingernails. 'You're all about to join the Free German Youth. Now, when you join the FDJ, you promise to support the DDR in the struggle against militarism. And we've been learning that the DDR is against countries which build up huge stocks of guns and tanks and other weapons.'

Paul Sehr, on the front row, sat up straight and stared at the teacher in the same way he stared at all his teachers. It was meant to be a sign that he was concentrating. Herr Klein looked nervous, but he didn't stammer. 'What is the most evil weapon you can think of? I'm thinking of a weapon which doesn't only kill soldiers; it kills men, women and children, anyone who happens to be around.'

Paul Sehr's hand was ready to shoot up like a railway signal. 'The atomic bomb.'

Herr Klein nodded. 'Any others?'

Paul Sehr's hand shot up again. Everyone knew the answers. They had talked about militarism so often in other lessons. In geography, they learned about the countries in the world, like America, which built up huge stockpiles of terrible weapons. Herr Klein nodded at Paul when no one else put their hands up. 'Someone used chemical weapons last year, didn't they, sir? Like they did in the First World War. I think it was mustard gas, wasn't it?'

Steffi knew what he was talking about. 'It was the sort

which attacks people's nerves and makes them die in agony. They used it on a village where there were no soldiers, only old men, women and children.'

Herr Klein walked over to Steffi's desk near the window. He looked suddenly younger and stronger with the light falling on him. Steffi thought he was going to shout at her for speaking without putting her hand up, but he said, 'And do you know who's been supplying these countries with bombs, the sort of countries that use nerve gas on innocent people?'

Steffi was the only one in the class who knew the right answer to his question. But she had already been expelled from two schools and she didn't want that to happen again. She liked Hannah too much. So she smiled at Herr Klein and told a lie. 'America?'

Herr Klein didn't reply. He walked slowly back towards the front of the class, touching each desk carefully as he did so, as if that was the last he would ever see of the scratched old furniture and it had suddenly become infinitely precious to him. Then he sat down at his own desk and sighed. Nobody spoke. Herr Klein closed his eyes. He reminded Steffi of a sportsman before a big event, a weightlifter closing his eyes to concentrate before he lifts a heavy weight which might fall on him; or a skier going through in his mind all the risks he will have to take as soon as he has launched himself downhill. Then he opened his eyes.

'The DDR has become a major supplier of guns, tanks and the sort of chemical weapons which are used to murder innocent people.' He stood up. 'I think that's the most important lesson I shall ever teach you', he said. Then the bell went and he looked tired and old again, shuffling out of the classroom with his head bent like a prisoner tired out after a long, forced march.

There was no sound. Nobody knew what to say. It was only when they were out in the corridor, forced along by a stream of pupils heading for the playground, that Hannah spoke. 'Phew!' She looked around to check who was listening to them. 'I don't know why, but that felt like a funeral. I thought everyone was going to burst out crying.'

'I don't think it was sad. It was all right.' Steffi grinned, walking backwards and then hopping backwards so that Hannah thought she was going to fall down the stairs. 'It was more like a film I once saw, where a new baby was born. Everyone was worried and quiet and waiting and then it was suddenly all right. I bet Herr Klein feels good now he's got that off his chest.' She swirled round just as they reached the stairs and pushed her arm through Hannah's.

'It's funny really,' Hannah said. 'The way you were saying we needed one person to tell us the truth. And now we have. So I suppose now you're going to say everything will suddenly change for the better.'

'Nah!' Steffi jumped the last two steps, pulling Hannah with her. 'Herr Klein doesn't count. He's going to retire soon. It doesn't count as telling the truth when they can't do anything to him any more. I mean, he's betrayed us all these years and he's just making himself feel good by telling us all that before he leaves. They won't do anything to him.'

The next day Herr Klein wasn't in school. A heart attack, the teacher said he'd had. Steffi asked which hospital he was in so they could go and visit him, but the new young teacher wouldn't tell her. She said they didn't think he'd be having visitors. They said he didn't have long to live. Her name was Frau Wende. She asked them what they had done on the subject of militarism and they told her everything except the most important lesson Herr Klein had ever taught them. Frau Wende said that they hadn't learned very much.

The week after Herr Klein disappeared, Hannah's class were taken on a trip to a concentration camp. Hannah was glad they had a bus all to themselves, because she was ashamed at the rowdy songs a lot of her classmates sang. They sounded just as she imagined the Nazis must have sounded on their way to war. She felt sick as they drove along the road away from the village outside Berlin. Everyone was laughing and chatting and eating their crisps. One of the girls said, 'It makes you sick, these scruffy old buses they give us. The seats are really uncomfortable.' And Hannah thought of the people being transported along the same road fifty years before on the last stage of their journey, transported in dark, almost suffocating, smelly cattle trucks, boarded up so that the people in the villages couldn't see what was in them.

'It stinks,' whispered Steffi. For once they had been allowed to sit next to each other. 'How did they feel when they were driving along this road? Did they know they were going to die?' Hannah nodded. How had her mother felt as she was driving up to the border? Had she known she was going to die? Or was she excited? Had she really thought she could drive through to West Berlin as easily as if she were going through a traffic light on red? Did she think it was just a matter of looking both ways and convincing herself that there was nothing coming. Or was she scared, so scared that she felt sick?

They had learned all about concentration camps. They had learned how Hitler first shut all his political opponents in them so they wouldn't cause him any more trouble. Then the Nazis had filled the concentration camps with Jews and gypsies and homosexuals, and killed them just because they were Jews or gypsies or homosexuals—for nothing they had done, just because of what they were. They had put priests and nuns in the camps too, and anyone else who criticized Nazis or said anything bad about Hitler. At first, they had tried working people to death and then, when people didn't die fast enough, they had gassed them. Millions of men, women and children had been gassed or worked or starved to death in the concentration camps. In school, they had always learned that the murders had nothing to do with the DDR. They were told how the DDR was a new country set up after the war, whose people had never done anything wrong. And then Herr Klein had told them about the chemical weapons.

The road sign told them that the camp was five kilometres

away and Frau Wende started them off on another song. Someone burped loudly at the back of the bus and Frau Wende turned round. 'Mathaus!' she said. 'You're disturbing our song.' Everybody laughed and started singing again. Paper lunch bags rustled and Hannah heard the hiss of bottle tops being unscrewed from bottles of fizzy Buna Cola.

'What happened to all the Nazis who used to live round here?' Hannah whispered to Steffi. 'And all the people who saw what was happening and didn't do anything about it. Did they all go and live in the West?'

Steffi pulled a face and looked around. The song and the roar of the bus's tired old diesel engine were far too loud for anyone to hear what they were saying. She pointed at Frau Wende. 'Ask her,' she said. 'She'll tell you they all escaped to the West and went to work for the Americans.' Steffi's eyes widened in mock astonishment and Hannah knew she was about to do one of her imitations of the school Director. 'Haven't you forgotten, my dear?' she said. 'The DDR only celebrates its fortieth birthday this year. We didn't have anything to do with concentration camps. How could we?'

The bus slowed down and through its front window they saw the sign at the gate of the death camp, '*Arbeit macht frei*—work sets people free.' Frau Wende stood up and clapped her hands for silence. 'We're here!' Everybody cheered and raced to be the first off the bus.

There was a museum in the camp, where Steffi and Hannah managed to lose the others. While their classmates rushed from one photo to the next, keen to get out of the dark museum and into the bright sunshine outside, Hannah and Steffi took their time, reading the Nazi posters on the wall. Soon they were completely alone and the museum was quiet.

'Look at this.' Steffi had found a poster which the Nazis had put up everywhere when they were going to round up Jews in a city and transport them to a concentration camp. They read the words out quietly to each other.

Anyone who opens their door while Jews are being transported will be shot.
Anyone who looks out of their window will be shot.
Anyone who shelters a Jew or tries to hide him will be shot.
Anyone who fails to inform the authorities of the whereabouts of a Jew will be shot.
Any Jew seeking shelter with a German family will be shot.

The words exploded in the empty museum like the sound of bullets firing in the cold night air and Hannah felt tears scratching at her eyes. Her throat was aching. She stood there reading the words long after Steffi had moved on to the next exhibit. She wanted to say, 'In those days, they shot you for looking out of the window at the wrong time. Now they shoot you for crossing the road.' But there was no one listening.

Steffi came back and pulled Hannah towards a huge, black and white photo. A mother and her tiny daughter, both in long, black coats and with headscarves on, were being forced at gunpoint to walk in deep snow towards a big army lorry. 'This is worse,' Steffi said.

'No. The poster's worse.' Hannah pulled Steffi back to the poster that had once been nailed on every street corner and read it aloud to her again. 'It's much worse,' she said, 'because it's still like that now. We're not supposed to see anything or hear anything except what they allow us to see and hear. And we're supposed to inform the authorities immediately if we see anyone else doing something that's not allowed. It's just like today. It's OK to see what's wrong in other countries, but not here. We're not supposed to look out and see what's happening outside our own window.'

8

Berlin, June 1989

'I'm so proud of you all.'

Frau Wende was so proud that large tears fell on to her cheeks, bringing flakes of black mascara to stripe her orange, made-up face like a tame tiger. The blue blotches of make-up on her eyelids shimmered, but couldn't compete with the polish of the shiny red tip on her nose. She dabbed at her eyes and Ilke Oloff, who'd been fixing the black velvet bow around her neck for the last ten minutes, stepped back from the single, cracked mirror. 'Do you want to fix your face up, miss?'

Hannah stood with her back to the stairs that led outside on to the stage. She missed Steffi. She tried to see a pattern in the brown paint that was flaking off the walls like the peel off a mushroom, but there was none. She knew she didn't belong there, backstage at the Initiation ceremony.

There was only one light bulb working and Paul Sehr stood directly under it, tying Ilke Oloff's bow one more time. Ilke pulled away from him and stood on tiptoe to look in the mirror over Frau Wende's shoulder. 'No, that's not right.' The bow was once again untied. 'Only two more minutes,' Frau Wende said, grabbing the ends of Ilke's bow and tying it herself.

It was the first time Hannah had seen Paul Sehr in anything other than his Pioneer uniform. He was wearing a navy-blue jacket and trousers that were supposed to look like a suit but didn't quite match. Hannah felt stupid in her short black skirt and the white blouse which Oma had brought all the way from Leipzig because her father had said she could not wear her jeans to the Initiation. Hannah couldn't remember the last time she had worn a skirt. She watched the others pushing and shoving and brushing and combing each other in the crowded, dirty little room behind the stage. They had been talking about the new clothes they had bought for months. And yet all of them looked as if they were wearing clothes that belonged to someone else; shoes that were too big, or so small that they pinched and the pain had to be hidden behind a bright, festive smile; jackets that were so stiff they could have stood up on their own; and skirts that need never, ever be worn again, with any luck. The Initiation Day was the day they paraded in front of all their relatives and swore to be loyal members of the Socialist State.

Ilke Oloff put her arms around Frau Wende. 'Wish me luck.' She took one last look at her tie in the mirror. Hannah's Oma had wanted to curl her blonde hair the night before so she could wear it loose in long, flowing ringlets, but Hannah had resisted. She was the only girl who wore her hair as she did every day, in a single plait down her back. All the others were different people.

Frau Bruck opened the door from the stage and tripped down the creaking wooden stairs. 'Oh, don't you all look smart!' She wore a white blouse and a tight black skirt that made her stomach stick out in a curve like a black, velvet football. She babbled, like a tape-recorder played too fast. 'Don't they look smart, Frau Wende? They're ready for you, ladies and gentlemen. Goodness, I wouldn't have recognized you. Except for Hannah. Very nice, Hannah. Well, they're waiting. Let's go upstairs. Now remember, don't rush.' She tripped up the stairs so fast that she almost left the heel of her high-heeled shoe wedged in a chipped-off step.

'Mind that step. Mind how you go. We don't want anyone hurting themselves.' She took a breath after every second word. Then she disappeared through the door. They heard the floorboards creak and the echoing pitter-patter of applause as their form teacher walked across the stage to switch on the record player. The loudspeakers crackled and chairs scraped as they were pushed backwards and the audience stood up. The National Anthem began—there was a crack on the record.

By the time the National Anthem had finished, they were all up on the stage, with their hands by their sides and their eyes fixed on a point on the end wall which they had been taught to look at during the rehearsals. Only Hannah didn't fix her eyes on the back wall as they took the oath, promising to dedicate their hands and their hearts to socialism. Hannah made no promises. She looked down at the ground and mumbled words, any old words, staring at the red paper flags poking out of the tubs of ferns which hid the hours of polishing their shoes had had.

The cultural assembly hall of the People's Own Sewing Machine Factory, the factory nearest to Hannah's school, was dark and gloomy because the only light came from windows high up in the ceiling. Hannah couldn't make out the faces of the men in uniform sitting in the front row, only the red or green bands round their caps and the gold and silver braid on their uniforms. She couldn't see her father, or her uncle from West Berlin. She followed the lines of wooden folding chairs, with a bunch of red plastic carnations at the end of each row, but she couldn't make out anyone she knew.

It was supposed to be the most important day of her life. At least, that's what they'd told her at school—the day when she would become a full, grown-up member of the Socialist State. Hannah stared again at the shadows in uniform on the front row, the shadowy rows of shadowy faces and chairs dotted with red plastic carnations, and asked herself if that was all her life was going to be. And she asked herself when Steffi would have the most important day of *her* life, since Steffi had refused to join the FDJ or to go through with the Initiation.

The speeches droned on. Paul Sehr made a speech, talking, he said, on behalf of all his classmates. But Hannah didn't even notice he had been speaking until the thin sound of clapping hands in the echoing hall reminded her to stand up straight.

The last speaker was a man in uniform who tried to be funny. So people tried to laugh. He peered into the darkness of the hall and asked if they could throw a bit of light on the subject of this Initiation Ceremony. Then he went on talking while Frau Bruck whispered behind her hand and tiptoed around to different employees of the sewing machine factory, ducking so as not to block people's view of the stage and managing to look like a cat, chasing birds and always missing them, until she found someone to switch on the lights.

As soon as the hall was lit up, Hannah saw that they had red plastic carnations round the bottom of the lights. And she saw Steffi sitting at the back of the hall wearing huge black sunglasses and a green wig with hair that stood on end.

In the little room behind the stage where they had left their jackets, someone had drawn on the photo of Erich Honecker. He was standing, with his usual smile as wide as his huge, black-framed glasses, next to a woman from the factory who had her head down, working at a sewing machine. And someone had drawn him a moustache in red lipstick. Frau Wende wiped the picture clean with her handkerchief. 'We won't say anything more about this,' she said. 'Now run along and enjoy yourselves.'

Steffi was waiting at the door, her green wig swinging like a handbag in her hand. 'How did you get in?' Hannah had refused to give Steffi one of her tickets because Steffi had already shouted at her and called her stupid for going through with the Initiation.

'Paul Sehr gave me a ticket.'

'Since when have you been friends with Paul Sehr?'

Steffi smiled a sweet smile. 'I told him I was really sad that I wouldn't be joining the FDJ and he said perhaps they might let me have an Initiation next year. He felt dead sorry for me, Hannah. Honest.'

'Well, I hope you feel dead guilty.' Hannah started to laugh. 'What made you wear that wig?'

Steffi twisted the bright green wig around and said, 'It's beautiful, isn't it? I knew you lot were getting dressed up in strange things, so I thought I should, too. They wouldn't let me wear it when I arrived at the door, so I took it off and then put it back on again inside. Do you like it?'

Hannah shook her fist at Steffi and ran off to join Oma in Onkel Alex's big new Mercedes. The last thing she wanted was to hang around with the others in her new, uncomfortable clothes, having photos taken next to army officers.

After Onkel Alex had paid for their meal at the Palace Hotel they all drove back to their tiny flat. Each of them carried boxes and boxes of presents from the boot of his Mercedes up eight flights of stairs because the lift wasn't working again. There was hardly any room on the floor in their living-room and Onkel Alex was so big that Hannah was afraid he would punch holes in the walls every time he moved.

He had brought a whole box of bananas with him from West Berlin. You could hardly get bananas in the DDR, so even after they had eaten their celebration dinner in the hotel, Hannah still found room to eat two of them, before tucking into some of the special chocolate he had brought. Then Oma and Hannah sat down on the sofa, waiting to watch the film her uncle had made on his last visit, while her father hovered near the light switch, ready to switch on or off as soon as Onkel Alex gave the order. The last time Onkel Alex had visited them was more than seven years before, on Hannah's first day at school.

The light went out and Hannah saw her mother, smiling and kissing her and tying two hair ribbons on her plaits before someone read out her name and Hannah, with a new schoolbag from West Berlin that was far too big for her, rushed over to join her classmates on the school stage. Her new shoes were so shiny that she almost slipped on the polished floor.

The film showed a world Hannah had forgotten, a world where she was glad to go to school, happy and proud to be a Pioneer, a world where her mother and father weren't constantly talking about whether to move to the West or not, a world where her mother looked so young and happy that Hannah almost didn't recognize her.

84

Onkel Alex had bought one of the first cameras with its own soundtrack. They heard the squeak and the slipping, ripping noise as seven-year-old Hannah's new shoes made her almost lose her balance. A kind voice said, 'Careful!' and Hannah cried out, 'Frau Schmidt!' before her first teacher came into the picture, catching her hand and stopping her from falling.

Oma put an arm around Hannah. 'She was such a nice woman,' she said. Hannah was glad they were sitting in the dark. She knew that Oma was watching her and she didn't want to cry. She was afraid. She knew that if she started crying because of an old film showing her with her mother when she was seven, she would never stop. Everywhere in their flat, all around the streets of Berlin, there were reminders of her mother.

The children in Hannah's first class stood on the stage looking scared—all except Hannah, who smiled and twisted and turned and waved right at the camera. Then the teacher came on to the stage and they all fell silent, ready to sing, 'Little White Dove of Peace'. That was something Hannah remembered very well. She remembered because it was the first time she had ever met her Onkel Alex and she couldn't wait to rush home after the one short lesson they had that day and tell him what they had learned. Frau Schmidt had talked about the song, 'Little White Dove of Peace' and told them how the people in the DDR only wanted peace, whilst other governments like the government in West Germany spent a lot of money on guns and war.

Hannah remembered how she knew that her uncle came from West Berlin. But she didn't know that West Berlin was part of West Germany. So she had rushed home and, while she sat on Onkel Alex's knee, told him about the picture of a soldier they had had to draw. Then she had told him what a bad country West Germany was. Onkel Alex had got very angry with her mother and father and told them they were stupid to stay in the DDR. And then he never came to visit them again.

Onkel Alex must have remembered, too. He switched the film off after the song. The room was dark and quiet. 'How can you stay here after what they did to her?' he said. Hannah heard him blowing some dust off the projector and then there was a whirring noise as he rewound the film.

Hannah's father switched the light on. 'We have to be realistic. It would be almost impossible for us to leave, after what she did.'

'After what she did! What did she do? All she did was try to drive from one end of a street in Berlin to the other. Where's the harm in that?' He didn't look at Hannah's father, but concentrated on winding the cable round the hooks on his projector. 'You've got to leave this place. You've got to get out—for Hannah's sake. She's got her whole future ahead of her. Do you want her to end up like her mother, so sick of it all that she doesn't care what happens to her as long as she gets away?'

Oma squeezed Hannah's hand, but Hannah didn't feel sorry for herself. She was too worried about her father. She wanted to protect him against her strong, rich uncle, who talked as if he knew what was best for them. He didn't understand what their life was like. He only saw the bad things about the DDR. 'Papa would lose his job the minute he applied to leave,' she said. Her father loved his work in the theatre. 'And anyway, we don't really want to leave. Oma and Opa live here. My friends are here. We belong here. Why should we want to leave?'

Onkel Alex opened his case and stowed the projector neatly away next to his camera. 'Well,' he said, 'no one can force you to leave here if you don't want to.'

No one was forcing Hannah to join the FDJ. Steffi told her that every day. 'You don't have to join, you know. They won't put you in prison if you don't join.' Hannah didn't want to join, but everyone said that if you wanted a good job you had to join the FDJ. Steffi just didn't seem to care what sort of a job she got.

Hannah sat outside the door, waiting for the test she had to take before she was accepted into the the FDJ. Frau Wende had told her not to worry about the test. 'Everybody passes,' she said. But that was what Hannah was worried about. She didn't know if she wanted to pass or not. There were two other girls before Hannah and both of them had their noses in their Citizenship books. Hannah had left her book at home. She hadn't even looked at it in the two weeks since Onkel Alex had left. She had agreed to have her Initiation because she said it was a good excuse for having a party. She had thought that a visit from Oma and Onkel Alex would cheer her father up. But everyone who went through with the Initiation joined the FDJ.

She had told Onkel Alex that you had to become a member to get a good job or to go to university. But she knew that it wasn't enough just to be a member. You didn't only have to join; you had to work really hard in the FDJ and then afterwards you had to become a member of the grown-up Party. Hannah knew that she didn't want to spend her life doing what the Party wanted her to do. She wasn't even sure if she wanted to go to university if that meant working for the Party as well.

The second girl went into the test room. Hannah stared at the picture of Erich Honecker, but his empty grin and the eyes behind his black-rimmed spectacles told her nothing. She stuck her tongue out at him, thought for a moment that there might be a hidden camera right behind the picture and then did it again. Then she had a bright idea.

She knew that if she refused to join the FDJ as Steffi had done, her father might get into trouble. But if she did so badly in the test that they wouldn't let her join, then nobody could blame her for not belonging to the organization. Hannah decided to fail the test.

A green light went on above the door. Hannah went into a very small room. Two men and a woman in uniform were sitting behind a desk and there was just room for one small swivel chair in front of it. Hannah sat down. She soon realized that she wouldn't have to try very hard to do badly in the test. She really didn't know the answer to at least half of the questions and found herself swaying from side to side on the irresistibly swivelling chair. 'Er. I'm afraid I don't know that one. We did it in class, but . . .'

The woman was satisfied. 'Well, as long as we know she's done it at school, she should be all right.' Hannah tried saying absolutely nothing, and the woman said, 'Well, we'll leave that one for now and come back to it later.' But they never did. At least ten questions were brushed under the table and forgotten. Hannah even tried giving what she knew was the wrong answer, but the woman only said, 'I see. What you really meant to say was . . .' and gave her the right answer.

After Hannah had spent twenty minutes doing her best to fail, the three examiners looked at each other, nodded and then smiled at Hannah and shook her hand. 'Congratulations,' the woman said, 'you are now a member of the FDJ.'

When Hannah went to Steffi's house for the first time, she asked Steffi why she didn't go to a school nearer home. Steffi's house was huge, and miles away from their school, but Steffi mumbled something about the local schools not being suitable. The house had belonged to Steffi's grandmother and she and her family had lived there for the last ten years. They had taken a lodger since her father moved away, but there were still only three people in a house with four bedrooms and two living-rooms.

'Your mum's not in the Party, is she?' whispered Hannah. People who were something important in the Party sometimes had more rooms than they needed.

'Are you insulting my mum?' Steffi stood in the large kitchen, hands on hips, challenging Hannah to repeat what she had just said.

'What's she saying about me?' Steffi's mother didn't look at all like her daughter, except for the clothes whe wore; a short black skirt and T-shirt which Hannah had seen Steffi wearing at school.

'She asked me if you were something big in the Party.' Steffi's mother rolled up the cloth she had been using to clean the table and pretended to throw it at Hannah.

In the afternoon, two families came to visit, each with three children. 'Now you know why I'm always hanging round the Alexanderplatz,' said Steffi. 'It's quieter in the city than it is here at home.'

Steffi's mum served out a cake she had made with gooseberries from their garden. 'It's our anniversary today,' she laughed. 'We've been waiting ten years for a phone. But they say they can put one in next month.'

'I think you're better off without a phone,' said one of the men.

Steffi's mum sighed. 'Well, at least you don't have to assume you're being bugged. It's awful at work when I go on the phone. I mean, you automatically lower your voice when you need to say important things.'

'Like talking about the elections,' said Steffi.

Hannah understood now why Steffi knew so much about politics. She lived in a different world to Hannah, a world where people told each other the truth—about their own feelings and about the state of the country. None of the grown-ups were afraid to speak—even though they didn't know Hannah. They said what they thought in front of her. Hannah felt as if she were listening to people speaking a foreign language and was surprised at how much she could understand.

The tall man was called Wolf. 'I don't drop my voice when I talk about the elections on the phone,' he said. 'It's the only way I can protest. And if I don't protest, I'll burst.'

His wife carried on, 'He phones his mother every night and says things like, "Do they think we're stupid? Why do they bother telling us that 98 per cent of people voted for the Party when they know we did our own count and we know the elections were rigged." '

The only people Hannah had ever heard criticizing the government before were her mother and Onkel Alex. It felt different when the people at Steffi's house talked. They didn't want to prove that the DDR was a terrible place as her Onkel Alex did. They didn't want to run away from it, as her mother had done. They wanted to make it a better place to live. Some of their friends had been put into prison because they had protested about the election results, but still they weren't afraid. They were talking about organizing a demonstration to demand new elections.

Hannah sat with her feet up on a chair, her arms hugging her knees. She was sure they wouldn't be allowed to organize a demonstration, but she was excited. The people at Steffi's house made her feel that something could be done. Steffi took a biscuit from the table. 'I want to show you something,' she said.

Hannah took her plate with the gooseberry cake and followed her. On her way upstairs she said, 'This is what you are looking for, isn't it? People who speak the truth.'

Steffi nodded. 'But I've told you already. That lot in the kitchen don't count. I've known them since I was little.'

Steffi had a pile of newspapers on her bed. 'That's illegal,' Hannah said. 'You're not supposed to keep newspapers.'

Steffi grinned. 'Yeh. They don't want you to notice that what they say today is the total opposite of what they said two months ago.' She shook her dark brown curls. 'We decided that if ever they searched our house we'd say my mum needs them for papier mâché.' She opened a cupboard, piled full of even more newspapers. 'I'm looking for March,' she said, 'the end of March.' Hannah sat on Steffi's bed eating her cake.

'I'm looking for the article we saw about your mum.'

Hannah put the plate with the half-eaten cake carefully on Steffi's desk. 'You don't need to look in the paper,' she said, 'I know what happened. I could have told you. Why didn't you ask me?'

'Do you know what really happened?' Steffi sorted through the papers, adding each one to the pile on the floor after she had glanced at the date.

'Of course I do. She was my mother.'

Hannah saw the bullet wound again, her mother's white face drained of blood, and she told the lie she had rehearsed often before. 'My mother tried to drive straight through a checkpoint without stopping. It was a stupid thing to do. She had no chance. She must have known she would end up in prison. But we hadn't seen her for such a long time, you see. We don't know why she did it. They shot at her tyres, but her car didn't stop; it skidded out of control and crashed. They said she died instantly. Anyway, I don't want to talk about it.'

Steffi ignored her. 'Did you read what they said about it in the papers?'

Hannah shook her head. 'We didn't get the paper for weeks after she died.' Hannah put out her hand and touched the paper which had come out the day after her mother died. She wanted to see what it said, but she knew it would tell lies and she didn't want to read any more lies. 'It's probably rubbish.'

'Read it.' Steffi turned to page seven. There was a very short article, just six lines of one column. A reckless driver had caused a lot of damage at a border control point. The article said that the driver was possibly drunk. There was no mention of the driver attempting to leave East Germany to drive to the West. No one mentioned that.

Hannah pushed the newspaper away. 'It wasn't like that, was it?' said Steffi.

Hannah shook her head, 'I've told you. I don't want to talk about it.'

Steffi put the newspaper away and started to bundle all the other papers into a cupboard. 'I'm not stupid,' she said, pushing several newspapers in with every word she spoke. 'We read all about it in West newspapers as well. I know what they did to her.'

'I know what they did to her because I saw it.' Hannah's head pounded and she felt panic rising in her, as if Steffi was about to hit her with a clawed hammer.

'I thought I was your friend! Why don't you trust me?'

'I don't want to talk about it. I don't want to talk about it. I don't want to talk about it.' Hannah stepped backwards away from Steffi.

'All I want to know,' said Steffi, 'is why you keep trying to become one of them. Why did you join the FDJ?'

'I did my best not to.'

'Well, go to the office and resign then. Hand in your pass. You don't belong with them and the Party after what they did to your mother!'

Hannah wanted to go home. She had a hot, burning headache and she felt sick. 'Why don't you just leave me alone?' It did her good to shout at Steffi. 'You keep telling me I should make up my own mind instead of letting other people decide things for me. So leave me alone and let me make up my mind.' She slammed Steffi's door and threw herself downstairs, glad that the laughter from the living-room was so loud that nobody heard her leaving.

Hannah's father hadn't expected her home before he left for the theatre. He went into the kitchen to warm some milk. 'I'll make you a hot drink,' he said. The evening was so warm that Hannah didn't feel like a hot drink, but she didn't say anything. After they shot her mother, Hannah had noticed that her father started to do little jobs that she was perfectly capable of doing for herself, like making cocoa. It was as if he tried to do things which pleased Hannah, because he couldn't think of anything to say to her.

'Papa.' Hannah leaned against the side of the kitchen doorway, watching her father as he stirred sugar and cocoa powder together with a spoonful of milk.

He looked up at her and then stared back into his pan of milk, as if it would boil over the minute he looked away. 'Hmmm?'

'Did you know what they wrote about Mama in the paper, after they killed her?'

He shook his head. 'I didn't want to read the papers. I know the sort of thing . . .' He poured the hot milk into two mugs, stirring it slowly.

'Did you know they said she was a reckless, drunken driver?'

Her father handed her a mug of cocoa and then blew on the milk in his own. It was the beginning of June, but he warmed his hands on the outside of the mug as if he was freezing. 'They sent me a bill for the damage they said she did with the car.'

'How could they?' Hannah banged her cup down on the low table near the sofa. 'They were the ones . . .'

'I had to pay it, Hannah.' Her father put his cup down slowly and put his arm round Hannah. 'It was all part of the bill for the funeral they wouldn't let us go to. I had to pay it.'

'It was good that we didn't go to the funeral,' said Hannah. She hugged her father and buried her face in his grey cotton shirt. 'We might have given something away. We might have cried when we weren't supposed to.'

9

Berlin, June 1989

After they shot Chinese students in Tiananmen Square, Hannah did cry. She was all alone at home, watching West German TV when the news came and with it the pictures, images Hannah would never forget, of students sitting peacefully in the Square. That was all they had done. Hundreds of students sat down in Tianamen Square and asked for democracy in China.

Hannah sat in the old brown-brocade armchair which had always been her mother's when they were together. She saw the tanks, seeming to roll incredibly slowly as if in slow motion, but still catching up with the running students, shooting them in the back as they tried to get out of the Square. For a second, it looked as if the tanks would stop for a young man who tried to talk to the men in control of the guns and tanks, but they shot him too and his body was tossed aside like a scarecrow. Hannah didn't know she was crying, but the tears wet her face and neck. She didn't notice what the rest of the news was about or that the news had finished and a game show was on the air. The clapping was like the rattle of machine-gun fire.

Steffi was dressed all in white the next day, because she said that was the Chinese colour for mourning. 'They'll do the same to us,' she said. 'Except that here in the DDR, they'll make sure nothing gets filmed. They won't let TV cameras anywhere near the place when they decide to shoot us.'

After school, Hannah went to Steffi's house and at night they watched the news together. First they watched the West German news and heard how people all over the world had condemned the Chinese government for the shootings in

Tianamen Square. Then Steffi switched over to the East German news. Someone from the government was being interviewed, Egon Krenz, the man Steffi said looked like the wolf who ate Red Riding Hood. He smiled at the interviewer, showing a row of sharp, yellow teeth. 'Of course, we have to offer the Chinese government our support,' he said. 'They were forced to clamp down on an extremist minority.' Steffi growled and snapped off the television.

'Come on,' she said. 'We're going out.'

'I have to go home,' Hannah said. 'Papa doesn't like me being away at night, even when he's out at the theatre.'

'We'll be back long before he gets home.' Steffi was already outside the door. 'Come on, I'll make sure you get home in time. My mum'll be mad at me too if we're late.'

Hannah only saw the boy from the side because he didn't turn round when they entered the church. He kept his eyes fixed on the hands of the drummers. Down at the front of the great, red-brick church, near the altar, men and women with small, thin drums between their knees beat out a protest which echoed round the knave and up to the high, arched roof. Sometimes their hands were raised up as if they were going to join them in prayer and then they beat down flat on the skin of the drums. Sometimes the beating was hard like the hooves of a horse hitting a road and sometimes it was as gentle as a heartbeat, so that the sound was almost lost on its way up to the balcony where Hannah and Steffi had found a place. The boy kept staring at the drummers' hands; flying, beating, stroking hands. Hannah looked around her at the crowds of people. The last time she had seen such crowds was during the Whit concert of the FDJ. At that time, Steffi had called them Rent-a-Crowd because they had all been paid to go along and pretend to be merry.

This crowd was different. They were silent, listening to the drummers. Sometimes Steffi would grab Hannah's arm and point to a man with a small leather shoulder-bag and whisper,

'Stasi'. Then her shoulders would scrunch up as she giggled silently. 'What's the use of a secret police who can never keep themselves secret?'

Hannah watched the boy's face. He had hair that was shiny and curled and dark red-brown as a chestnut when it first comes out of its case, but she couldn't see what colour his eyes were. She wanted him to speak to her. She couldn't imagine ever having the courage to speak to him.

'They're drumming in protest at what happened in Tianamen Square,' Steffi said in a very loud whisper, after they had been sitting in the church for at least ten minutes. 'They're funeral drums for all the people who were killed there.'

The boy turned round and Hannah saw that he had dark brown eyes. 'They're drumming for us,' he said. 'We're the next ones they'll use tanks and guns on.'

The boy's name was Simon and he had just left school. 'They wouldn't let me stay on,' he said. 'I'm Jewish and I didn't want to join the FDJ.' He went outside with them and they started walking along the road towards their bus-stop.

'What were you doing in an Evangelical church if you're Jewish?' Steffi laughed. 'I told you, Hannah. You meet all sorts at these church meetings.'

Hannah kept quiet. She had never been inside a church in her life before. Her Oma and Opa in Leipzig went to church, but they had never taken her with them.

Simon laughed too. 'I've got a job here,' he said. 'That's how I found out about these meetings. You don't have to be Evangelical to come to the Peace Group.'

'I thought they'd put you in a factory if you didn't want to join the FDJ.' Steffi was never nervous when she met someone new. Hannah wished she could think of something clever to say to the boy, something that would make him notice her. But he was too interested in talking to Steffi.

'Nope. They wouldn't even have me in a factory. The priest here gave me a job, and I'm going to study at evening classes. I want to be a doctor.'

Steffi whistled. 'They'll never let you do that if you don't join the FDJ.'

Simon shrugged his shoulders.

'Anyway, what is this great job the priest has given you?'

They reached their bus-stop and Simon grinned. 'I'm a grave-digger. Just look at my muscles.' For a moment he held up his thin right arm, trying to show biceps like a body builder. Then he waved and walked off back towards the church.

'I thought he was coming this way to get a bus,' said Hannah.

'He just wanted to make sure you got to the bus-stop safely,' said Steffi. Then she sang out, 'I think he likes you.'

'I hate you,' said Hannah.

The next day, the careers adviser came to their school and interviewed everyone in Hannah's class. Hannah's interview was over very quickly. She told the woman she wanted to be a doctor and the careers adviser, writing in a red register, put the word, 'doctor' next to her name. Then she told Hannah she would have to go regularly to the FDJ to make sure she learned everything she needed to be a good doctor in the Socialist State.

Steffi told the woman she wanted to be a clown, but the careers adviser didn't write that down in her red book. She told Steffi she was putting her name down for an apprentice-ship at the nearby sewing machine factory. 'She said I should have something to fall back on.' Steffi went round asking everyone in their class and all the other classes with pupils of the same age. Every single one of the girls who was not eligible to go to university had been put down for the sewing machine factory.

Hannah scolded her. 'You could go to university if you joined the FDJ,' she said, but Steffi laughed.

'I could go to the West if I wanted to go to university,' she said. 'I told you. I want to be a clown. That's what this country needs.'

10
Berlin, July 1989

Hannah had never wanted to take Steffi home to her flat. Steffi's house was big and in a posh part of Berlin, while Hannah lived in one of the tower blocks in the centre, like most of the other children in their class. Whenever Steffi asked her where she lived, she usually just pointed over the school wall in the right direction and said, 'Over there.' In between the school and the blocks of flats was a museum and a row of smaller, prettier houses. Hannah hoped that Steffi would think she lived in one of those.

The flats hadn't been built for very long, but the lifts never worked and the lights on the stairs were always broken so that you had to climb up eight flights of stairs in the dark to get to Hannah's flat. And to make things worse, there had been a fire in a flat on the fourth floor the year before. No one had ever come to fix the flat afterwards. The outside walls were still blackened from the flames and charred, tattered curtains flapped at the broken window. The flat where Hannah lived was nice enough inside. But she didn't want Steffi to see the ugly, broken building.

Then, one night, after Hannah's father had left for work, someone rang the bell five times and Hannah peered through the spyhole. It was Steffi.

Hannah grinned and shouted, 'How did you get here? Hey! Where did you spring from?' all the time she was fiddling with the heavy chain her father had fitted to the door. She wasn't angry with Steffi for coming. It was a new feeling to have a good friend, someone who cared about her and wanted to come and see her. She hugged Steffi.

'I was dying to see you. I wanted to tell you. I'm so glad you've come. I couldn't wait until school tomorrow. My father wants to send me off on a summer camp again this year—FDJ.' She groaned. 'He says I need the company and he won't have me sitting on my own at home all summer.'

'Me, too.'

Steffi unlaced her boots, pulled off her socks which were far too thick for a July evening, and curled up on the old brown sofa, just as if she had always lived in Hannah's flat. 'My mum's coming to get me later on,' she said. 'She wants me to go off to a camp as well, but I've told her I'm not going. Yeuck! Do you remember Pioneer camps?'

Hannah stood to attention and recited the words she remembered saying every morning for four weeks every summer since she had started school. 'It's my duty to love my country, my parents and my teachers . . .'

'And it's my duty to always wash myself!' Steffi threw a cushion into the air and they watched it landing behind the sofa. 'We always had to say that standing in line outside our huts. I mean, it was really early in the morning and they made us rush out of bed and stand to attention and recite all those things that make you a good socialist. At our camp, we always had to wash in freezing cold water and they used to tell us it was good for us.'

'We had it much worse,' said Hannah. 'We had to do early morning exercises, really hard so that you ached all day. And they called that a holiday!'

'I bet our early morning exercises were worse than yours. Oh, Hannah, I can't go to one of those camps again, I can't, I can't.' Steffi turned and buried her head in the saggy old cushions and drummed with her feet on the arms of the sofa. Then she sat up straight again. 'No. I'm definitely not going. I've just remembered the Military Instruction. No. I'm not going through that again. I bet you didn't have Military Instruction. I mean, fancy going on a summer holiday to have Military Instruction. No!'

Hannah wrinkled up her nose. 'We had Defence Theory. We had to run around the woods throwing pretend grenades and stuff. And then they showed us these boring films about people in the army. Paul Sehr loved it.'

Steffi nodded. 'I bet they were the same films we had. They said we had to learn to defend ourselves because the people in the West are always wanting to attack us and one day they will. Oh, Hannah, wasn't it boring?'

'We did learn a bit of First Aid.' Hannah got up off the floor and went into the kitchen. She wanted to see if there were still two bottles of Buna Cola in the cupboard. When she found them, they were warm, so she had to take the milk out of the fridge to make room for them. She thought Steffi was asleep when she went back into the living-room.

'I used to like the camp fires,' she whispered, slipping down on to her mother's strange sheepskin rug that must have come from a dark brown, very woolly sheep. They didn't have a fireplace in the flat, but she closed her eyes and imagined all her friends sitting in a circle huddled round the camp fire. Sabina had been with her the last time she had been at a Pioneer summer camp.

'The songs were a bit stupid,' Steffi whispered, her eyes still closed. 'All those Workers' Marching Songs. But I used to love the camp fire.'

'We used to take turns cooking,' whispered Hannah.

'Yeh. We used to swap with the teachers so that they had to be kids for a day and we got to boss them about and make them do early morning sport. Mmm. The camp fires were lovely. I can just smell the sausages grilling.'

'We used to go for trips out. And one day our bus broke down. But nobody minded. Everyone sang songs and even the teachers told jokes.' Hannah sighed. 'It was nice.'

'I used to fall asleep sometimes, in front of the camp fire,' whispered Steffi. 'I used to ask my mum could we have a fire in our back garden, but she always said it was too dangerous.'

They were quiet. Hannah could almost hear the gentle crackle of the camp fire and see the light glowing on her friends' faces. She had always come home happy from the summer camps.

Then Steffi sat up and shouted, 'Why are we whispering? I

am not going to any old summer camp and that's that!' She lay down again on her back and folded her arms.

'I'm going to try and persuade my father to let me go to Leipzig instead, to my Oma and Opa.'

'I'll come with you.' Steffi sat up again. 'Please, Hannah. Please, please! Let me come with you to Leipzig! My mum's got to go to some conference and I just know she's going to incarcerate me in a camp.'

'I don't mind. Do you want a drink?' Hannah emerged proudly from the kitchen with the two Buna Cola bottles. They didn't often have drinks like that. Someone at the theatre had given them to Hannah's father in exchange for a couple of light bulbs. 'Opa and Oma won't mind. I'll see what my dad says.'

Steffi switched on the East German TV news. She turned the sound down and did a perfect imitation of the blonde woman newsreader's voice. 'Erich Honecker today visited the People's Own Needle Factory in Blumenstadt where they reached their production target for the fifth year running. He presented them with a silver-framed photograph of Erich Honecker. Erich Honecker today also visited the People's Own Spoon factory in Blumenstadt, where they reached their production target for the tenth year running. Erich Honecker presented them with . . .'

'Oh, shut up!' Hannah switched over to the West German TV news. Another blonde woman newsreader was talking about the hundreds of people who were trying to leave East Germany by taking refuge in West German embassies abroad. There was a film of hundreds and hundreds of people coming out of West German embassies, waving their passports or sitting on narrow beds lined up in rows in what the newsreader said was a school sports hall in a small West German town near the border.

After the news was over, they switched the television off. Steffi was quiet. Then she got up and opened the door which led from Hannah's flat out into the corridor.

'Is anybody there?'

Her voice echoed round the landing, down eight flights of stairs and up the remaining seven. But there was no reply. She tried again.

'Is anybody there?'

There was no answer.

'Hannah,' Steffi giggled, pushing her back inside the flat.'Everybody's gone to West Germany. We're the only ones left.'

Hannah could never go to sleep until her father got home from work. Even when she was tired and went to bed she never slept. After Steffi had gone, she sat on her bedroom floor, pulling one book after another off the shelves. She felt like reading, but she didn't know what to read. She had read almost all her books, all except the ones her father had brought home for her in the months after they shot her mother.

Hannah knew that her father brought children's books home because he liked to read them himself. She could tell that because he still kept on bringing picture books long after she had learned to read books without pictures. One of the new books was the kind she really liked. It was called *Romances from Tadshikistan*, and it was full of beautifully painted pictures. Papa said the pictures gave him ideas for work.

The stories were all about Princesses and their fathers, the Padischas, and about the trials princes had to go through to marry the princesses. One story was called, 'The Black Slave'. When the Padischa heard the prophecy that his daughter would one day marry a black slave, he made sure he gradually moved all the black slaves from his country. But he missed one slave, who lived far away from the palace. The slave won the contest which would have granted him the hand of the Princess, but the Padischa invented one more test for him to prove he was worthy to have the Princess's hand in marriage. Then the Padischa thought up another test and

then another. Finally, at the end of the last test, the black slave met a sorcerer who promised him his skin would turn white, and he would please the Princess and her father, if he bathed in the water of a wondrous lake. The black slave decided he had had enough of trying to please the Padischa and his daughter and he certainly didn't want to change the colour of his skin for them. So he went away and didn't marry the Princess. Hannah liked that story best of all.

The black slave was like Steffi in the end, someone who was brave enough and clever enough to do things because he wanted to, someone who didn't want to change himself to please other people. Simon and Steffi were both like that.

The next day, Hannah went along to the headquarters of the FDJ. 'I want to hand in my membership card,' she said to the man on the desk at the front entrance.

'Oh, no, young lady.' He shook his head and looked sorry for her at first as if she were suffering from heat stroke. 'It doesn't work quite like that. Oh no. You've got to follow the right procedure.'

'I just don't want to be a member any more. Can't I just hand in my card?'

'Oh no, it's not that easy. If it were that easy, everyone would be doing it, just because they're too lazy to go to the meetings. You've got to follow the right procedure.'

Hannah felt like giving up and going home. 'What do I have to do, then?'

The man at the door shook his head. 'It's not easy. You have to go to the right office and take an oath. You took an oath when you joined. You can't get out without taking an oath in front of the right authority. It's got to be official, see?'

'Which office do I go to?' Hannah didn't want to put off her decision. She felt that if she didn't resign that day, she might never resign.

'It's not in this building.' The man behind the desk spoke slowly, as if he had a large, juicy sweet in his mouth and it was going to drop out if he wasn't very careful with his words.

Hannah took a deep breath. She had learned never, ever to

get impatient with the people who let you go in or out of an official building. 'Can you tell me where I have to go, please?'

The man stuck out his tongue in his cheek and then rolled his tongue around his mouth as if a gob-stopper was stopping him talking. 'That depends how serious you are about this. I mean, there's the Young Persons' Office, where you can go if you just want to talk about it. Perhaps you don't like someone in your brigade or something . . .'

'No, it's not like that,' Hannah said. 'I just want to resign.'

'Ah well, then you have to do it official. Follow the proper procedure. You'll have to go to the Town Hall.'

At the Town Hall, Hannah found out that the lawyer who had to be there to take her oath only worked in the mornings on Monday and Friday. She had to wait for three more days, and the lawyer made her feel like a criminal, but still she didn't give up. By Friday afternoon, Hannah was no longer a member of the FDJ.

But she didn't tell anyone, not even Steffi. Not even when they travelled alone together all the way to Leipzig to spend the summer with Hannah's grandparents.

11

Leipzig, August 1989

'Your mother used to play at making walls,' Oma said. Hannah and Steffi were helping her to make apricot dumplings for their lunch and the girls sat at the kitchen table stoning apricots while Oma rolled out the dough. 'I've got some photos of her somewhere. She was about four when they first started building the Wall.' She shifted the dough round and shook some more fine, white flour on to the table.

Steffi licked her fingers. 'Mmm. These are good. You get such good things to eat in Leipzig. I've never seen apricots in Berlin.'

'Opa gets them from his friend,' said Hannah. 'You're supposed to be stoning them not eating them. Oma's counted them, haven't you?'

Oma said, 'I'll need at least twenty-four. You count them for me.' Then she started cutting up the dough into squares. 'Twenty-eight years. You wouldn't believe it, would you?'

'Ugh! They never stop going on about it,' groaned Steffi. 'Twenty-eight years since they built the Wall. Forty years since they founded the Socialist State. They live on anniversaries. What I want is one year where they don't go back twenty-five years to find out something marvellous happened. I mean, why don't they try making something wonderful happen in my lifetime for a change?'

Oma grabbed a handful of apricots and started to stone some herself. Then she formed the dough into a round bag around each one and twisted the bags at the top to seal them. The water was almost boiling.

'Hurry up with that job,' she said. 'We want to have them ready before Opa comes back from his rehearsal.' Hannah's

Opa played viola in a big orchestra in the city. 'We all thought the Wall was a marvellous thing once,' Oma said.

Steffi was just about to put another apricot into her mouth. 'You what?' She let the apricot drop on to the pile next to Oma's.

'We really thought the Wall was a good thing. That's why we took all those photographs. I've got them somewhere. I'll find them for you afterwards. Photos of Hannah's mother playing at building walls with blocks left lying around by the soldiers. We were so proud of her and the other children. They looked so sweet building walls like the soldiers.' Oma sat down. 'We were still living in Berlin then.' She screwed her nose up, mimicking Steffi's still horrified face and smiled. 'They told us we were keeping the enemy in the West away from us, my dear. And we believed them.'

She finished off the last of the dumplings and let them slide into the gently simmering water. 'It was only afterwards that we realized the Wall was built to keep us in.'

'But everyone knows they were shooting people then,' said Steffi. 'I mean, even while they were building the Wall, they were shooting anyone who tried to get over it. And you still thought it was a good thing?'

Oma took her apron off and started to brush the flour from the table on to her hand. 'We lived a long way from the Wall in Berlin,' she said. 'Not everybody lives right next to it. We didn't get to hear about the shootings on the Wall from the radio and we didn't have a TV then. All we knew was that too many people were leaving to work in the West and that our country was being drained of all its wealth.'

Steffi was quiet then for a long time. But she couldn't remain quiet. There were things she had to know. She didn't know what questions to ask, but she couldn't keep quiet.

'And after they shot Hannah's mother?'

Hannah looked at Steffi as if she had pulled out a pistol and threatened to shoot Oma. She had never, never asked her grandparents any questions about her mother's death. She didn't want to hurt them. Hannah didn't want Oma to cry. It was the same with her father. She always felt that the best thing was to keep quiet and not ask questions. Oma stood with her back to them and stirred butter and sugar into the breadcrumbs in a saucepan, until the butter melted. 'Oh,' she said, making a very long O sound, and taking her time as she stirred and stirred in the saucepan. Then she added some cinnamon to the mixture and the kitchen was filled with the smell of warming spice and sugar.

'Oh, we knew,' Oma said. 'We knew what was happening at the Wall long before they shot Hannah's mother. We've been trying to pull down the Wall for years, fighting against the people like Erich Honecker who say it will stand for another hundred years. We were fighting the people who built the Wall long before they shot my daughter. And we won't give up now.'

'Oma never wanted to leave the DDR,' Hannah said proudly. 'She's like my father. She says if we want things to get better here, we've got to stay here and make it better.'

'Your mother never wanted to leave either,' said Oma. 'That's why she became a teacher. She thought she could change things, if she was a teacher.' She turned her back on them again while she drained the apricot dumplings and piled them on to one of her huge blue and white platters. They heard Opa's key in the lock.

'I'm hungry,' said Steffi.

Hannah sometimes felt as if everything that happened in the world took place on television and not in real life. When they turned on the television at night, West German TV was full of reports of what was happening in her country. But Hannah never actually saw any of the things that were reported while she was on her way to school or while she was staying in Leipzig. And nothing was ever shown on East German television. For all she knew, West German TV might be making up all the stories of the hundreds and hundreds of people leaving East Germany every day. Perhaps they were just showing films of the same people, over and over again.

She couldn't really believe that so many people were leaving. Another couple of pupils from her class had left after Sabina went. But they might have just moved to another part of East Germany. No one ever said that they had gone to live in the West. Hannah could understand Oma saying that people hadn't realized what was happening when they first built the Wall. If nobody told you at school. If it didn't come in the newspapers or on the television, how could you know about the shootings that went on? Unless it was your mother they shot.

It was so quiet that Hannah could hear Opa's deep, regular breathing. His eyes were closed, but Hannah wasn't sure if he was sleeping or not. Steffi sat with her legs crossed like a tailor, squashed in the high wing chair at the end of Opa's long narrow study and pretended to read a newspaper. After a while, she sighed, put down the paper and tiptoed in her bare feet over the shining wooden floor to where Hannah was sitting on the window ledge. She stood for a long time looking over Hannah's shoulder at the very old pop-up book which Opa had only been allowed to read on Sunday when he was a child. Then she reached out her hand to pull at one of the paper levers which would make the baker beat the boy who had tried to steal his cakes.

'Hey!' said Hannah, forgetting to whisper. 'I'm reading this. You said you wanted the newspaper.'

'Sh!' Steffi still had her hand on the pop-up book. 'It's so boring. Nothing ever happens here.'

Opa's eyes opened. 'Right, I'll take you both off for a walk. That'll cut the boredom.' He sprang from the sofa and started to fold the newspaper which Steffi had left on the floor.

'I didn't mean that,' said Steffi. 'I didn't mean it's boring staying with you. I meant, nothing ever happens in the DDR. Nothing changes. Everything good in the world happens somewhere else.'

'She's right, Opa.' Hannah wanted him to go back to sleep. He had to play in a concert that evening and she thought

Oma would shout at them for waking him. 'Things are never going to change here.'

Opa shook his head. 'I'll show you whether things are going to change or not. Go and tell your grandmother that I'm taking you with me tonight,' he said. 'Tell her not to forget the candles.'

Every time Hannah went anywhere near a church, she thought of Simon, the boy from Berlin who was digging graves because they wouldn't let him do his exams. She was sure he didn't think of her, but she couldn't stop herself remembering his brown eyes and his smile and the passionate way he had spoken of helping to make East Germany a better place to live. She was longing to talk to someone about him, but not to Steffi. Steffi might laugh at her.

It was dark inside and outside St Nicholas' Church when they got there after the concert, but the darkness wasn't threatening or sinister. It was a darkness warmed by thousands of candles and by the warmth of peaceful, welcoming voices. Hannah thought of all the times she had been in public halls or outside rallies where she had seen so many people and all she could think of was strained faces and voices, of people looking over their shoulders to see who was watching them. She thought of how Steffi had called out 'Rent-a-Crowd' at the Whit meeting of the FDJ, because everyone knew that hundreds of teenagers only turned up if they were paid.

It was different in the church. People were pleased to see each other, hugged each other and smiled as if they were at a private party, with no fear of being watched by the Stasi.

'There must be hundreds of Stasi here,' Steffi whispered.

Opa nodded. 'Oh, yes. But most of the other people are not regular churchgoers either. They come here because of the Peace March. It's the only place they can meet without being arrested.'

Steffi glared round at some men she thought were from the

Stasi. Somehow they looked ridiculous in the church, where no one was afraid of them. Many different people made speeches about peace before the priest came forward and told the huge crowd to carry the message of peace home. Then a young woman played the guitar and the congregation sang with her, 'We shall overcome.' Steffi and Hannah didn't know the words and couldn't understand how everybody could sing in English. No one learned English at school.

They were among the last to leave. Hannah carried the sense of peace and happiness with her as she watched the lines of candles in the procession in front of them, glowing in the darkness. She wished Simon could have seen the masses of people coming together, not afraid to let the government see that they wanted a change. In the *Nikolaikirche*, Hannah felt she belonged somewhere.

Hannah and Steffi didn't want to go back to Berlin after they had taken part in the Peace Demonstration. When Oma pointed out that they had to go back to school, they begged to be allowed to stay for at least one more march the following Monday. But that was the day they had to travel back to Berlin. On their last night in Leipzig, Opa didn't have to play in a concert and they sat together in Opa's study, watching the West TV news. Steffi was, as usual, sitting squashed up like a tailor in Opa's chair, while Hannah sat between her grandparents on the sofa. But Opa wasn't really paying attention to the news. He got out the girls' railway tickets and started giving them instructions about the bus they had to take to the station.

'Sh!' Steffi flapped her hand behind her, like a very unskilled bird preparing for take-off. 'Look. Listen. Sh!'

Opa stood with his hands on the back of Steffi's chair, looking as if he might fall over if he didn't have anything to support himself. Five hundred people. Five hundred people, the newsreader had said. And they had just walked across the border in full view of Hungarian soldiers and marched off down a country road into Austria. Five hundred people. The newsreader moved on to another subject.

'I missed it, I missed what happened,' Opa said. 'Tell me what happened. What time is the next news? I want to watch it again, to see what happened.'

Steffi told him. Five hundred people on holiday in Hungary from East Germany, mothers, fathers and children, had been taking part in some sort of festival, and there was a picnic at the end of it, out in the country near the border. Suddenly, a group of them had taken wire cutters to the border fence. As the soldiers approached with their machine guns, the people had just smiled at them and smiled at the TV cameras which were there from all over the world. And they had said to the soldiers, 'If you shoot one of us you'll have to shoot us all, men, woman and children, with the eyes of the world on you.'

Five hundred people had walked through the border between Hungary and Austria. And nothing had happened to them.

Opa picked the phone up. 'Now he'll be calling the whole orchestra all night,' said Oma. 'It's always the same, whenever something happens, he's on the phone for hours. Just you watch him.'

But Opa didn't dial any number. He stood there listening. Steffi and Hannah could hear voices as if Opa had got through to someone, but he hadn't dialled a number. They saw him smile and he tapped with his hand on the desk. Then he whistled quietly, still tapping on the desk. Finally he looked at his watch and coughed.

'I pay my taxes so this country can have a proper secret service, not a pile of bungling idiots who don't even realize that I can hear them after they've bugged my phone and pressed the wrong button.'

Then he put the phone down. 'You can tell your Papa that nothing much has changed in Leipzig. They'll still be listening in whenever he calls.'

111

12

Berlin, September 1989

'We're getting off the subject. We're going too far off the subject. Let's keep to the subject, please, ladies and gentlemen.' Frau Bruck had left. Most of the kids whispered that she had gone to the West, but they weren't allowed to whisper for long. A very old teacher had taken her place.

'He was the only one they could find,' whispered Steffi. 'Soon there won't be any teachers left except for old fogies like him.'

'Frau Bruck lied to us,' whispered Hannah. 'She said she would never, ever think of leaving the DDR. Think of all the people she forced to join the FDJ. It was her that made me think I had to join. And then she goes and lies to us like that.'

'All teachers lie,' said Steffi. 'It's part of their job. If you're a teacher, you have to lie.'

Hannah's mother hadn't wanted to lie. It hurt to have to lie, to repeat the same lie over and over. 'My mother was a teacher. She didn't lie.'

Herr Theobald prowled round the classroom like a mangy old, toothless old, bald old lion. He came to a standstill behind Steffi. 'And may we all share in the conversation?' he asked. His eyebrows blurred into the lines in his old, newspaper-yellow skin.

Steffi shrugged her shoulders. 'Which conversation was that, sir?'

His eyes were yellow and striped with threads of orange blood. His mouth sank in as if it was being sucked by perilous sinking sands. 'I don't like your sort of girl,' he said. 'You're the type who applies to leave the DDR as soon as you leave school. Get all your education here and then disappear to the West to make . . . money . . .' The word 'money' made

Hannah shrink away from him. The word 'money' leapt forward like a poisonous snake about to strike. 'You won't deceive me,' said Herr Theobald. 'I know your sort. Go and stand outside the door.'

Steffi spent most of her time for the next three weeks standing outside Herr Theobald's door. He told them that smog was the curse of West Germany because their cars were too big and too fast, and Steffi laughed out loud. Then he told them that smog stopped at the DDR border and that you could see the line where the smog stopped, running along the far side of the Wall and Steffi stood up and said, 'Rubbish.'

The next lesson, Herr Theobald told them that anyone who went along to peace meetings in churches ought to know that every single war in history had been started about religion. He said that the peace meetings were all part of a plot by the churches to start another war. And Steffi stood up and said, 'You don't know what you're talking about.'

Hannah admired Steffi. She wished she could stand up and say what she really thought. But she was always too scared. She didn't want anyone saying that she was the sort of girl who wanted to leave the DDR. She didn't want them to say she was just like her mother. She didn't want the new teacher watching her, as Frau Bruck had done, her eyes like a microscope searching for the tiniest fragment of proof that Hannah and her father had known about her mother wanting to escape.

Hannah was relieved when they finally started their two weeks' working practice outside school. They were supposed to learn all about life in socialist factories, but Hannah had been put in a hospital kitchen because she wanted to be a doctor. She saw a lot of the nuns who worked as nurses, but she never saw a single patient. For two weeks, she sweated in the hot, hospital kitchen scrubbing huge pans over a sink filled with such steaming hot water that she felt as if she was in a Turkish bath.

Steffi was sent to a clothing factory where loud, old-fashioned pop-music blared out of dusty loudspeakers the whole day, and where the workers had nothing to do except sit around on the packing cases filled with new machines. The new machines couldn't be used because the electric leads needed to plug them in hadn't arrived. And the old machines had gradually got more and more useless because there, and ten times more money than you get here.' Steffi factory told Steffi how there used to be a team of ten sewing machine mechanics on duty every day of the week. They had all gone to the West. 'There's good jobs for mechanics over there, and then times more money than you get here.' Steffi was bored and angry. By the end of the two weeks, both girls couldn't wait to get back to school.

It was Simon's idea to go on the Peace March on the 2nd of October. For once, Steffi seemed afraid. She said the whole demonstration would be bristling with Stasi, like a pincushion with all the pins turned the wrong way out. Simon wasn't afraid. He went to all the marches. He had even joined the protest group, New Forum, who were campaigning for democracy in the DDR. 'There are too many of us now,' he said. 'And the Press are there, from all over the world. The Stasi won't do anything. They can't do anything.'

Hannah was afraid to go because she was worried about getting home late. She had never told her father about her evening visits to the church and to the Peace Marches. She knew that he wouldn't have let her go, and besides, she was always home before him. The Peace March on October 2nd was different. It was due to start later than the others and there were lots more speakers, so that Hannah was almost certain to get home late. But she wanted to go because of Simon. He even said he would walk home with her after the march was over, just to make sure she got back in time.

Hannah and Steffi arrived early, but the church was already so packed that people were assembling outside on the lawn. 'We'll never hear anything,' Steffi said. The rows and rows of candles looked magical, flickering across the lawn and in a ring of people right around the churchyard wall.

Hannah saw bobbing flames dancing up above her head where people had climbed on top of the churchyard wall. The tiny flames danced higher and higher above the rest of the crowd. 'We'll never find Simon.'

'I know where he is.' Steffi grabbed hold of Hannah's hand and steered her through the crowds towards a door in the side wall of the church. The door opened when they knocked because Simon was standing right beside it. He caught hold of Hannah's hand and kissed it as if she were a princess.

'I knew you'd come.' His eyes were shining.

He went in front of them, showing them the way to the places he'd saved and Steffi nudged Hannah and grinned. 'See! He does like you!'

'I hate you.' Hannah frowned and then smiled. It was all too beautiful. There were no lights on in the church, but the whole building was brightly lit by the candles people were holding.

As soon as the service began, there was singing and laughter and speeches about how the DDR would only become a better country if everyone worked together. The Bishop talked about the people who were leaving for West Germany and said that leaving the country wasn't the answer. He talked about the schools which were short of teachers, and hospitals short of nurses and doctors, and begged everyone present at the Peace March to stay and help to rebuild their country.

Simon was elated. 'Who could think of leaving?' he said, as they slowly, very slowly followed the long procession out of the church. 'Why would anyone want to leave when there are so many people working for Peace in the DDR? The Stasi don't stand a chance now.' Hannah loved to hear him talk like that. Simon smiled at her. She hardly dared to believe that he liked her. He was the only boy she had ever liked.

The church was in a road with a whole row of foreign embassies, huge white houses with balconies and flights of steps up to grand front doors. The silent, candle-lit march moved past the houses as if one huge vessel were gliding through the streets instead of thousands of people. The only sound was of people's footsteps, quiet, slow footsteps. Hannah could hear her own breathing and blew out to make a ring of white smoke as her breath hit the cold air. It was so peaceful.

Then they turned the corner and heard the first sounds. There was shouting at first. It sounded as if someone had accidentally fallen down in the gutter and a few others had stumbled over them or were running around trying to get help.

Then Hannah heard the barking of Alsatian dogs. People all around them began to link arms, making one solid line across the road, and Hannah marched in the middle, her arms linked with Steffi on her left and Simon on her right. A woman screamed and the shouting and screaming grew louder. Hannah's candle fell to the ground and went out and there were too many people moving behind her and in front of her for her to stop and look for it. She had to leave it behind.

The crowd began to press backwards against them, as if someone up ahead was pushing them hard. And then more screaming started. 'They're setting dogs on us.' The crowd began to break up, the candles were extinguished and they were left in complete darkness: a darkness made horrible by people screaming in pain. Now there was the dull thud of wooden coshes, of people being beaten, quite close to where they were standing. The Peace March had become a trap.

'We've got to make a run for it.' Simon squeezed Hannah's hand. 'I'll see if I can find you both when we get out of this, but we've got to run. I'm sorry, Hannah, for bringing you here'. He started to push her and Steffi backwards, trying to make them see that the only escape was back the way they had come. 'I was wrong. I'm sorry. I thought the journalists from all over the world would protect us. But journalists are nothing to them. They still don't care what they do. Run for it, Hannah. Be careful.'

They never did find Simon again that night. Hannah was cold with fear. She had always been afraid of dogs and now she could hear the growling and barking of Alsatians coming closer. No one knew how many there were, but Hannah could tell from the screams and shouting that the dogs were attacking people. She heard loud, rough voices calling the dogs off and saw shadows struggling. The whole of the street was a mass of shadows.

Once they had lost Simon, Hannah froze. She was afraid of being knocked down and trampled under the feet of the crowd. She was afraid of moving forward in the direction of the dogs, snarling and leaping up at her. She was afraid to go back the way they had come. But the dogs were free. She could tell there was no one holding them on a lead. They were being allowed to attack people.

'I can't believe this,' said Steffi. 'I can't believe this.' At first her voice was very calm and steady, but that was no surprise to Hannah. She never expected Steffi to be afraid. 'I can't believe this.' Steffi's voice sank to a frightened whisper.

Hannah reached out for Steffi's hand. 'There's nowhere to go,' she said. 'They've trapped us and now they're going to set their dogs on us.'

Steffi shouted, 'No. No. I'm not staying here. Come on.' She tugged Hannah backwards and sideways, struggling through the crowd until they got towards the pavement. During the march, people had walked in the middle of the road and still in the midst of all the chaos the pavement was less crowded than the road. 'Run,' Steffi hissed, and they started to run back the way they had come, towards the street full of embassies, the street with the church at the end of it. 'We'll be safe in the church,' Steffi said. 'Simon must have gone back there.'

They couldn't run. They could hardly walk. But at least they were moving away from the cordon of policemen and police vans which had trapped the marchers from the front. They had nearly reached the corner, when a woman shouted, 'They've blocked the road up here too. There's police vans across the road.' The doors of all four vans burst open as soon as she shouted and the light from inside the vans blinded the marchers, who had got used to the almost total darkness.

'Down the side,' said Steffi. 'Come on, Hannah! Some people are getting through round the side of the far right-hand van. They can't get us all. Come on!' Hannah, still clinging to Steffi's hand, was yanked forwards, closer and closer to the police vans.

At first, when the police vans loomed out of the darkness and the doors were flung open, the crowd still kept on moving. There were so many marchers, and only enough policemen to fill four vans. But there were dogs in every van, greedy, fierce bullying dogs, and the policemen had guns.

The crowd began to draw back. Just in time, Hannah slipped through the gap between the door of the nearest police van and the high wall round the embassy at the corner of the street. She was ready to run on now, faster than they had been running before. She wanted to run as fast as she could and get right away from the crowd, but Steffi's fingers started to tighten on her hand and she felt herself being dragged backwards, back towards the open door of the van. It was like one of those terrible nightmares she had had ever since they shot her mother, dreams where she was running and running, trying to get away from something awful, something behind a high white wall that towered above her. Her feet were trying to run but she wasn't moving forwards. And the nightmare creatures were getting closer and closer.

Steffi pulled and pulled at Hannah's hand and Hannah tried and tried to pull her forwards, away from that awful place. Hannah didn't know why she wasn't moving. Like Hannah's nightmares, there was no sound at first, only the feeling of panic because she was running and running and not moving.

Then Hannah heard the savage growling. And Steffi was sobbing quietly. 'Help me, Hannah. Help me. It's got my arm.' She cried like a baby and the dog growled and snapped as if it was playing with a bundle of rags. Hannah wanted to cry. She wanted to look round and plead for somebody else to help them. But people were too busy trying to get away. Steffi stopped crying and just stared at Hannah. They didn't want to shout. They didn't want a policeman to come, the only one who might have made the dog let go of Steffi's sleeve. Hannah grabbed hold of the iron bar that hung loose through the door handles when the van wasn't being used to transport prisoners.

Later that night, she thought she must have been crazy, but at that moment, all she could think of was that she had to get home before her father did, so he wouldn't know she had been out at the march. She didn't think of what the dog would do if it turned on her. She forgot she was so afraid of dogs that she always crossed the road if she saw one. If the police caught them, they'd have to go and answer questions and her father would worry about her. They had to get away. She lifted the iron bar and shoved it in the dog's mouth, forcing it to let go of Steffi's arm at last.

'Come on!' Hannah whispered, keeping one eye on the dog as it growled and worried at the iron bar. 'Run, Steffi. We've got to get away.'

Hannah had heard about animal bites. She knew there was some illness you could get that could kill you if you didn't get to hospital after being bitten. And the dog had torn through Steffi's sleeve and into her arm.

Steffi was crying and shocked, and her breath came in short gasps. 'I can't go to hospital, you idiot. The hospitals will be crawling with Stasi. Whoever they didn't get at the march, they'll round up at the hospital.'

Hannah was in control. 'We can go to my hospital. It was all nuns there. It's a church hospital. There won't be any Stasi. And we can go round the back way—through the kitchen.'

Sister Impetua swooped along the polished green linoleum of

119

the hospital corridor towards her kitchens. She had cooked in the hospital kitchens for the last thirty years.

'I've never known a night like this one,' she said. Her keys, on the chain attached to her brown leather belt, jangled in time with her steps.

Doctor Fuchs nodded and tried to keep up with Sister Impetua, as if walking quickly would help him to keep awake. He had only just finished his training, and had been on duty for forty-eight hours with only a few hours sleep in between.

'It's never been so bad that they've had to call me in to casualty before. My job's always been in the kitchens.'

'The boss said a lot of them were dog bites. What do you make of that? And head wounds.'

Sister Impetua didn't know what to make of the dog bites. It was as if a horde of wild animals had suddenly been set loose in the streets. She wouldn't have been surprised if she had heard on the news that there had been a mass breakout at the West Berlin Zoo and the wildest animals had leaped over the Wall. She pushed through another door, swept past the sign that said Children's Ward and was a good way down the corridor by the time Doctor Fuchs caught up with her.

'There just aren't enough doctors and nurses.' Sister Impetua's words got lost on their way back to the young doctor, but he nodded in agreement with everything she said. 'All the nurses who aren't nuns seem to have got it into their silly young heads that they have to leave the country and go and live in West Germany. I don't know why. There are too many nurses in West Germany.'

Sister Impetua slammed open another swing door and sailed through, letting it shut with a soft thud behind her. She passed the sign pointing to the hospital chapel and made the sign of the cross. Then she waited for Doctor Fuchs. 'They say there are nurses in West Germany having to work as cleaning women because there are no jobs for them. Couldn't we do with them here, what with people's relatives having to come in and give them a wash and getting under the nurses' feet, most of them?'

Doctor Fuchs nodded. It was the same with the doctors. The hospital had lost seven doctors in the last month and the new young ones like Doctor Fuchs had to work so hard that they didn't know how to keep awake half the time.

'They were talking about a Peace March, some of them with bites on their legs.' Sister Impetua pulled a large white handkerchief out of the deep pocket in her long, brown wool skirt and blew her nose. She didn't think much of people who went marching through the streets. Up to no good, some of them.

'I don't know about a Peace March. It didn't look very peaceful the state most of them were in.'

Doctor Fuchs was so tired that the pale green walls and the dark green polished floor flowed into one another and the whole of the long, long corridor went up and down like a ship in a storm. His own voice sounded far away when he talked.

'There's still one emergency operation going on,' he said. 'I've dealt with three cases in collapse. Just stopped breathing. I'd better grab my cup of tea and get back there. I thought the walk would do me good, but . . .'

'You need to sit down for a while.' Sister Impetua was well aware that there was only one doctor left to attend to all the people with gaping wounds in their heads. And there were nurses running round searching for syringes to give injections to people who had been bitten. Sister Impetua had counted the syringes only the day before. She knew they wouldn't have enough. She pushed open the swing doors marked Staff Only.

There had been police barging in as well, with their rough loud voices, grabbing hold of people who were sitting in the casualty department waiting to be attended to. And Sister Superior had spoken to them very quietly and asked them to leave and they had gone. Quite right, too. This was a church hospital, not a police station.

Reporters, too, there had been. The cheek of them. One young man had limped in holding his right leg, taken a seat in the waiting room and then pulled a camera out and started filming the patients sitting there waiting to be seen by a doctor. Sister Superior had shown all the reporters to the door. There had never been a night like this one at the hospital in all of thirty years. Sister Impetua quickened her pace, her keys ringing out a warning that she was approaching.

And then finally, things had started to get a bit quieter. Two of the operations were over and the two doctors and theatre sisters could get to work on the rest of the patients in casualty. And Sister Impetua had been allowed back to her kitchen to get on with what she did best—making tea and coffee and hot soup. She pushed open the swing doors marked Hospital Kitchen and reached up to get her long apron from the row of hooks beside the door. Then she turned round.

'Hannah! Lord bless us! Did you come to help us in our hour of need? We're that short of nurses, I had to help out and Monika's gone on holiday with her family, so I'm on my own in the kitchen. The good Lord only knows whether she'll come back or not, with times like they are.' Her eyes fell on Steffi.

Steffi couldn't stand up any longer. Every time she tried to stand, she saw lights spinning before her eyes and knew she was going to faint. She sat on the bench behind the huge kitchen table, with her head resting on her arms. There was a loud noise going round and round inside her head, as if someone had built a motorway in her skull without asking her permission. She looked up at Sister Impetua and thought she was seeing a ghost, a ghost in a long green apron.

'She . . . she didn't want to bump into the police,' Hannah explained.

Sister Impetua sighed. 'I don't know what the world's coming to, I really don't,' she said. 'And I thought you were such a good girl, Hannah.'

It was two hours before the doctor and Sister Impetua

finished with Steffi, giving her one of their last injections and stitching up the wound in her right arm. They wanted to keep her in for the night, but Steffi said she felt fine. 'My mum hasn't got a phone, you see,' she said. 'I've got to get home.'

There were no more buses, so Hannah walked all the way to Steffi's house, taking the extra long way round after they had left the hospital by the back door. She thought of phoning her father but remembered the Stasi listening on Opa's phone. It was no good letting the Stasi know where they all were. If she could only get Steffi home, everything would be all right.

After the bright, warm hospital kitchen, it felt very dark and cold outside. But at least it was quiet now. Hannah knew Berlin and she knew the streets they could take to avoid trouble. She put her arm round Steffi's waist and Steffi leaned with her good arm on Hannah's shoulder. And as they kept on walking, Steffi seemed to revive and gain more strength.

'I never told you why I was expelled from my first school, did I?'

The streets were absolutely empty, not a car in sight, but still they stopped at the traffic lights and waited until the light with the little red bear flickered off and the little green bear gave the sign that they could cross the road.

'I never asked you,' said Hannah.

Then Steffi told her about the posters that went up in her school asking for an end to war, and the petition she had signed and the way the Stasi had been brought in to investigate. She talked about Hannah's mother, her art teacher, and how she was the only teacher who had looked upset on the day they were expelled. 'I wasn't actually expelled,' Steffi said, as they turned into her street and saw her house. 'I was like your mother, I suppose. The whole place made me so sick, I just had to stand up and leave. But it was easy for me to leave the school. No one was going to shoot me for doing that.'

Steffi's mother drove Hannah home. 'Do you want me to come up with you?' she asked.

Hannah shook her head, 'It'll be all right.'

It was after midnight and Hannah's father still wasn't home.

13

Berlin and Leipzig, October 1989

Hannah and Steffi should have been too scared to set foot outside the house after Steffi was bitten at the demonstration. They should have realized that the police and the Stasi were too powerful. They should have known that a crowd of people, armed only with candles and protest songs, didn't stand a chance against policemen with automatic guns and fierce dogs. They should have been worried, after Simon had disappeared, that they were the next ones on the list of hundreds to be taken away and locked up by the Stasi. After the nightmare of that last demonstration, they should have decided that they would never, ever go near a demonstration again.

But they weren't scared any longer. There were more protest meetings planned in Berlin, because President Gorbachev was going to visit the city for the Fortieth Anniversary of the DDR. Steffi and Hannah knew there would be even more policemen out in the city for Gorbachev, and hundreds of extra members of the Stasi. But still they wanted to go to the demonstrations. Steffi even went along to the headquarters of New Forum and told them she was going to make a speech at the demonstration on the 6th October. She wanted to tell people all about Simon disappearing.

Steffi had heard kids in their class saying that nobody cared about the bad things that happened in the DDR. But she knew that wasn't true. People did care. They just didn't know. They were never allowed to know. She was determined to let them know about Simon.

'You're a bit young,' the woman in the New Forum office said. 'You're putting your head on the block if you speak at a demonstration. They take photographs of you.' Then she shrugged her shoulders. 'But you're probably on record already. They take photos of everyone who comes into this office.'

'I'll wear a wig,' said Steffi. 'My mum's got lots of wigs.'

'Listen, at some demonstrations they arrest people as soon as they leave the platform.' The woman didn't smile.

'I'm a good runner,' Steffi said. 'I'm not afraid.'

'Leave it with me,' the woman said. 'We'll let you speak if we can give you protection.' Steffi and Hannah didn't want to wait until the people at the office could guarantee protection. They called at the New Forum headquarters every day, until a man finally told them they would get a chance to speak. Hannah shook his hand.

'Oh, thank you, thank you. If only enough people get to hear about Simon, we can organize another march. They'll have to tell us where he is if enough people know that he's gone missing. Won't they?'

The man took off his glasses and polished them on the frayed floppy edge of his dark green woollen cardigan. 'We're doing all we can,' he said. 'But he's not the only one who's gone missing. Just be patient. And don't forget to tell your father and your mother if you're coming to the demonstration. You should really get them to sign one of our forms, you know.'

They had forgotten Hannah's father. The night of the last demonstration, he had come home half an hour after Hannah and she never knew where he had been. But she knew that, whatever her father was up to, he would never give her permission to go on a demonstration. He came home one afternoon to find Steffi and Hannah in the living-room, trying to write Steffi's speech.

'Doing your homework?'

Steffi tried to shuffle the papers together into a pile to hide the top sheet, but Hannah's father had already seen the heading that Steffi had written proudly, in large red letters. 'Demo, 6th October.'

'Oh, no.' He shook his head slowly and picked up the pile of papers. 'Oh no, you don't. I've told you, Hannah.' He folded up the papers without looking at them and put them into his briefcase.

'I know what you're trying to do, Hannah. I can understand why you want to take part in the demonstrations. But I'm not having you getting yourself arrested. After what they did to your mother, they don't need much excuse to say that I'm an unfit parent and shut you away in a children's home. Anyway,' he smiled, 'I've arranged for you to go and stay with Oma and Opa for half-term, just about the same time as the fortieth anniversary. I'm sure they'll have Steffi to stay as well.'

Steffi shook her head. 'Can I have my speech back, please? One of us has got to go to the demonstration. Someone's got to speak up for Simon, and all the others they arrested.'

'Your father doesn't know much about your Opa and Oma, does he?' Steffi said later, as Hannah walked with her to the bus-stop. 'I mean, he can't know anything about them if he's sending you to Leipzig to get you away from the fortieth anniversary demonstrations. He must think they sit around in their armchairs drinking coffee.'

Hannah grinned. 'Mama knew what they were up to, but she never told him. He just thinks Opa's too old for demonstrations. I don't think I ought to tell him yet, do you?'

By Sunday, October 8th, everyone in Leipzig knew there had been demonstrations in Berlin. But it was only on West German television that they heard how hundreds of people had been arrested. Oma worried out loud the whole day about Steffi, until Hannah had had enough. 'We can't do anything to help her by worrying, Oma,' she said. 'Perhaps she's all right.'

Hannah worried about Simon too, but she never said anything. They had only ever met him at the church, and they

127

had no way of knowing whether he had turned up at home after the demonstration. He might be perfectly all right. He might have just decided that it was too dangerous to leave home. But still it was strange that there was no message from him.

On the East German news that night, party leaders spoke for the first time about the demonstrations. A general was interviewed and asked if the government had any intention of taking action against the troublemakers who were out on the streets demonstrating.

'They've already taken enough action,' Oma grumbled and went on folding the ironing. 'Look what that pack of savage dogs did to poor Steffi's arm.' Oma hadn't forgiven Hannah for not bringing Steffi with her for the half-term holiday. She was convinced something terrible had happened to her over the weekend.

'We shall certainly take action,' the general was saying. He sat up straighter in his chair and stared straight at the camera. 'And if we have to we'll use guns.'

'Right, that's enough,' said Oma. She unplugged the iron and switched the television off. 'They think they can frighten us. They think they can make me decide to stay at home instead of going on the Peace March tomorrow. Well!' She picked up her knitting, a pullover she was making for Opa, and started to knit faster than Hannah had ever seen. 'They won't frighten me.'

Opa and Hannah had already left the house the next day when the telephone calls started coming. Oma didn't answer the phone at first. The whole of the morning she stayed in bed and listened to it ringing. She had been sick all night, and stayed in bed trying to get better, determined not to miss the march.

Later on in the afternoon, Oma got up out of bed, but still she didn't feel like eating. The phone rang again while she was in the study writing letters. The woman at the other end of the line sounded out of breath and frightened. 'Thank goodness I've got through to you,' she said. 'I've been trying to contact someone all day. Your husband plays in the orchestra, doesn't he?'

Oma sat down and put the top on her pen. 'Yes?' She thought the woman was going to tell her that Hannah or Opa had been injured. After all they had heard on the news, she was ready for anything.

'I can't tell you who I am,' the voice said. 'But people told me your husband was the best one to speak to. He has to pass the news on to the whole orchestra and to the congregation in the church. It's urgent. They've been ordered to give out ammunition to the soldiers.'

Oma held her breath while she slowly unscrewed her pen top. Then she started to doodle on the pad next to the telephone. She didn't want to say anything. She thought of the Stasi who sometimes listened in to their telephone conversations. But this time, when she had lifted the receiver, there had been no tell-tale click. Perhaps they were lucky and there was no one listening in. Perhaps all the Stasi were involved in the preparations to stop the Peace March that night. Oma knew it was going to be one of the biggest marches they had ever had. She wrote 'Weapons' and 'Ammunition' on the pad and drew spiders' webs all around them.

'Are you still there?' the woman said. 'There's no one listening, is there?'

'I don't think so,' said Oma.

'The Stasi are going to be mixing with the crowd.' The woman's breath raced faster then her words. 'They're going to cause trouble in the crowd, to give them an excuse to shoot.'

Oma pressed so hard with her pen on the paper that she made a hole in the next two sheets. She wrote, 'Shooting into the crowd.' Then she asked, 'How do you know all this?'

'Look,' said the woman, 'I can't tell you who I am, but soldiers in full uniform have been seen going into sports halls all over the city. And they've come out the other side in civilian clothing. And Stasi. Leather bomber jackets and jeans. You know what they look like.' Oma was just about to interrupt. She wanted to ask the woman again, 'Yes, but how do you know all this? Who are you? Who do you work for?' But the woman went on talking.

'They've given orders for the hospitals to prepare 2,500 litres of blood. Hundreds of beds have been made ready. They've been sending people home if they aren't very ill, just to clear the beds. The kindergartens are going to close at three instead of four, to get the children off the streets. The police have been issued with gas masks and riot gear. You've got to warn the marchers.'

'They wouldn't do it.' Oma drew two straight lines under the words she had written on the notepad. 'Everyone knows about the Peace Marches by now. The eyes of the world are on Leipzig tonight. They won't want another Tiananmen Square in front of all those TV cameras.'

'There are no TV cameras. Western journalists have been forbidden to enter the city today.' The woman hung up.

Oma sat by the phone with the receiver pressed to her ear, staring at her piece of paper. She didn't know what to do. She had always believed that her government wouldn't shoot innocent people. Until they had shot her daughter. She still believed that no government could order soldiers to open fire on a crowd of innocent civilians. But governments were doing that all over the world. And now her government was preparing to fight a war against its own people.

She put the phone down and her ear was burning where she had pressed the receiver up against it. She tore off the top piece of paper from her writing pad, crumpled it up and threw it into the waste-paper basket. She sat there for a long time, hoping she would wake up and find that what the woman had told her was not true. She forgot about feeling sick and sat there paralysed, not knowing whether to go to the church or to the place where the orchestra rehearsed. She thought about phoning someone, but she didn't want to risk

130

being overheard. When she finally came to her senses, it was nearly four o'clock. The room was almost dark. She decided to go and look for Hannah and Opa in the orchestra rehearsal rooms.

The musicians had finished early. Every single one of them had left to go to the demonstration in St Nicholas' Church. 'What's the church's phone number?' Oma asked, but the caretaker shook his head as if she was stupid.

'That's not my job, being a telephone directory,' he said. 'I have eough trouble, making sure these people switch all the lights off after they've finished playing.'

Oma saw police vans on her way to the church, hundreds of them. Every second vehicle was a police van. She grumbled to herself because she was so slow with her walking-stick and then scolded herself out loud for wasting her breath talking. She saw crowds of people in front of her heading for the church and passed them by when they stopped to buy candles at the shops in the narrow streets around the church. She could have warned each one of them separately, could have told them before they ran into the trap the police had set. But she didn't know whom she could trust. It was always like that in the DDR. She saw young men carrying shoulder-bags and with leather jackets over their jeans and was sure they must be from the Stasi. But perhaps they weren't. She couldn't trust anyone. She couldn't tell anyone.

She thought she was the only one who knew of the bloodbath the police were planning, and yet she couldn't tell anyone. If she told the wrong person, she would simply be arrested and would disappear until the whole thing was over.

The streets were so full that she could hardly move forwards. People weren't pushing. They were kind and considerate and held her arm if she overbalanced and had to lean on her walking-stick. But there were just too many people. Thousands and thousands of people were shuffling towards St Nicholas' Church. Thousands of people were going to get shot. Oma felt faint.

She caught hold of a young woman's arm, a woman with

wild, black curly hair just like Steffi. 'Excuse me,' she said, 'Can you help me? We've got to let someone know. Someone in there.' She nodded towards the huge, red-brick church that towered above them at the corner of three narrow streets. Then she looked into the young woman's eyes and she was suddenly afraid. There was no one she could trust.

She closed her eyes and thought she heard the screams as bullets were fired into the crowd. She opened her eyes and the face of the young woman was blurred and grey. The church was falling towards them. She knew she was going to faint and there was nothing she could do. As she fell down, she thought she remembered the young woman shadowing her through all the cobbled streets from the rehearsal rooms to the church.

She felt herself being carried. Her eyes wouldn't open, but Oma could feel that she was being carried away, above the crowd. She heard voices buzzing and then fading away like people clapping in a concert hall and was sure that she was being taken away to one of the waiting police vans. She let herself go limp. There was nothing she could do.

When she regained consciousness, there was a heaven of white above her. White ceilings soared away to meet delicate red-brick arches. The high white walls looked cool and peaceful and calm. She was inside St Nicholas' Church, near the altar, and Opa was leaning over her. 'A nice trick to play,' he whispered.

Hannah stroked her hand and said, 'You've got us the best seats in the whole church, Oma, right near where the priest's going to be talking. It was a good thing we arrived just as they were taking you in. Opa thought you were dead.'

'I've seen people faint before,' Opa said. 'Of course I didn't think she was dead.'

Oma sat up. 'There's something I've got to tell you. Only it's too late now, and I don't know what we're going to do. I should have got to you before. I tried. The police are going to shoot everybody. They're going to open fire on the crowd. And they've got blood transfusions ready and everything.'

132

Opa stroked her hand. 'We know all that. It'll be all right.'

Oma was shaking. 'How can you say it'll be all right? They've got extra beds ready in all the hospitals.' She started to cry.

'It'll be all right,' Opa said.

The priest was the last person to give a speech, and he said that the only thing he could do was to wish people a safe journey home. He begged them not to become violent if anyone tried to provoke them. 'And there are people outside, wanting to take part in this Peace March, just so that they can make trouble,' he said. 'There are even people here in this house of God, who are here only to cause trouble. They are here to cause trouble even at the risk of killing innocent women and children. Let them be warned. We will put a wall of peace around anyone who wishes to make war on us.'

More than fifty thousand people took part in the march. The police paced up and down, threatening the crowd as caged lions try to threaten the visitors in a zoo, but they didn't move in. And no one was hurt.

When Hannah's father met her at the station, she told him she hadn't done very much during the week in Leipzig. When he asked her what she had been doing, she shrugged her shoulders. 'Oh, you know, the usual,' she said. Opa and Oma usually read a lot and Opa usually took Hannah to the concerts he played in.

'Didn't you hear anything of the demonstration?'

Hannah shrugged her shoulders. 'Just rumours.'

But the day after she got home, the television news from the West carried its first report about a demonstration in Leipzig. The newsreader said that more than ten thousand people had taken part.

'She doesn't know what she's talking about,' said Hannah. 'There were more than fifty thousand people there.'

Hannah's father switched the television off. 'Hannah. You've been lying to me. How do you know that?'

'I wasn't lying. I told you. We did the usual. Opa took me to the Monday evening Peace March.'

Before she had finished speaking, Hannah's father was on the phone. He snatched at the numbers as he dialled and got the number wrong twice before he finally got through to her grandparents.

Hannah could hear Opa at the other end of the phone. She wondered whether the Stasi were listening, but her father didn't seem to care. 'How could you?' Hannah couldn't hear what Opa said, but her father shouted down the phone and shook the receiver. He was so angry, she could almost imagine him taking her grandfather by the collar and shaking him. 'How could you take her there? I sent her to you because I thought she would be out of trouble. I could have kept her in Berlin if I'd wanted her to risk her life on a demonstration. Didn't you know the police had orders to shoot? You could have been killed, all three of you.'

He listened for a while and then put the phone down. He shook his head as if someone had just punched him on the jaw and then sat down beside Hannah on the sofa.

'Do you know what he said to me?'

Hannah shook her head.

Her father put his arm around her. 'I wouldn't like to lose you, my Hannah. I had to shout at him. Do you know what Opa said?'

Hannah shook her head and cuddled up close under her father's arm, feeling his heartbeat and hearing his voice, deep and gentle, reverberating through his chest. 'He said he knew that they had orders to shoot, but the march had to go on. He said you all just had to go ahead with it whatever happened. I had to shout at him, Hannah. God, I'm so afraid of losing you.'

'I know what he means,' Hannah said. 'I'm not afraid any more. None of us were afraid on Monday and we had to show them we're not afraid. We had to go through with the march.'

14
Berlin, October 1989

'Your father's up to something,' Steffi said.

Hannah didn't hear what she said. Steffi's face looked as if someone had been let loose on her with a whole box of face-paints in shades of purple, blue and green. She had a huge bandage round her right hand.

'What have they done to you? My God, Steffi!'

They met at the entrance to the church. Steffi had called Hannah as soon as she got back from Leipzig and asked her to help set up candles and decorate the altar for the next peace demonstration. Every Monday now, in churches all over Berlin, all over East Germany, more and more people got together to sing and pray for peace and talk about what East Germany could be like if only the government could be changed. After seeing how angry her father was that she had gone on the march in Leipzig, Hannah was even more scared about telling him that she was going to the peace demonstrations. All she could do was to make sure she got home before he did.

'Steffi! Don't just ignore me! What did they do to you.'

The huge church door groaned as Steffi pushed it open with her shoulder. It shut behind them with a hollow bang and they stepped on to the cold stone flags inside the empty church.

'Your father was on the demonstration at the weekend. Nobody else can get here till later,' Steffi said, 'so I said we'd make a start on the candles. There's a lot to do.'

Hannah hardly noticed what Steffi said about her father. She was disappointed. Every time they went to the church, she was disappointed to find it empty. She always half-expected Simon to open the door for them, or to be there in the vestry, sweeping the floor. She had asked Steffi on the phone if there was any news of him and she was too scared to ask again. She didn't want Steffi to tease her and say she was in love with Simon. She wasn't in love with him. She just missed him. Steffi strode over to the vestry and unlocked the door.

'Come on, Steffi. Who did that to you? Why are you ignoring me?'

'I'm not ignoring you. Can't you get the candles out? And the big, tall candlesticks.' Steffi staggered backwards, dragging a sheaf of branches which had been pruned from the beech hedge along by the road. She let the branches fall near the altar and stood up straight.

'These bruises are my souvenir of forty glorious years of East Germany,' she said. 'We had our usual peace demonstration in here and there were so many people outside that they had to use microphones wired to the outside so everyone could hear. What we didn't know was that all the time we were in here, they were already arresting people outside that door.' Then she stretched her arm right out and pointed to the door with the first finger on her right hand, so Hannah could see that it was only her finger and not the whole of her hand which was swathed in the bandage. 'They got us as we went out.'

'But Steffi, you look terrible.'

'It was terrible. But other people were much worse. That's why there's no point in talking about it.'

Steffi laid the beech branches, with their red-gold leaves, on the white linen altar cloth, overlapping so that the edges of the altar were covered with a golden crown of leaves.

'Simon's gone to Hungary.' She stood back to look at the altar and then stepped forward again to move one of the branches. 'But he may be in West Germany by now, if they gave him a visa at the West German embassy.'

Hannah stood still at the other side of the altar. It was as if a complete stranger had come up and violently punched her in the stomach for no reason.

'You're lying!' she shouted. 'Simon would never go to the West. He isn't the kind who'd run away. And anyway, he said he wouldn't. He said he was going to stay here and change things. I hate you for saying things like that!' She put the candles down and glared at Steffi's bruised blue and purple face.

'He could have stayed if he and his brother had wanted to go to prison, but there's not much you can do to change things if you're locked up.' Steffi took the candles, one by one, and placed them along the front of the altar in their holders. 'You don't know what it's like, Hannah. They kept me in a police cell for a couple of hours until my mum came to get me. She knew I'd been at the Peace March, so she came looking for me. Someone else told her about the police moving in, when all we were doing was singing in a church. I was lucky, Hannah. She got me out before they got round to questioning me. But I heard what they did to some of the others. You don't know what it's like.'

Hannah picked up a candle and forced the end into one of the holders near the lectern. 'Simon wouldn't leave,' she said.

'Hannah, while I was sitting in this cell, squashed up with six other girls, we heard a woman screaming because they were beating her up. The Stasi were beating everyone up. And we heard them shouting at people while they hit them. They kept on shouting the same things, getting louder and louder to drown the crying. "You so-called Peace Marchers always say we're Nazis. Well, now we'll show you what the Nazis were really like." I was frightened, Hannah. And I was only locked up for two or three hours. Simon and his brother disappeared for over a week. Their mother and father had no idea where they were. And when the Stasi finally let them go home, their parents decided to leave.'

Hannah didn't want to look at Steffi. She didn't want to show that she was crying. 'But Simon wasn't afraid of them,' she said. 'They'll never get me to be afraid of them any more.'

The sun had slowly gone down and the church was in complete darkness. Steffi started to light the candles and slowly other people began to arrive, all of them lighting their own candles from the ones on the altar.

There was no preaching at the peace demonstration that night. There were no political speeches made by the leaders of the New Forum group who wanted to change the government in East Germany. It was the 29th October, 1989 and East Germany was the same as it had been for years, only worse. The shops had even fewer goods for sale so that people had to stand in even longer queues every day to buy the food they needed to eat.

The hospitals were short of medicines and syringes, so that people were becoming gravely ill for want of an injection. They were short of doctors and nurses and relatives were looking after their own sick. The factories were short of the parts needed to repair machines, so that people had to stop working for days while their machines were mended. The factories with working machines were short of the people to work them. People were arrested and disappeared for days, phones were tapped and everywhere the Stasi watched and hid and found more people who were prepared to betray their friends for money. It was the same as it had always been, only worse.

Except that one thing had changed. First of all in small groups in the churches, and then in ever larger groups, and then even outside the churches, people were beginning to tell the truth. Hannah remembered how once, soon after she had met her, Steffi had said that East Germany would be a better place if only they could find one person who would tell the truth. And she remembered what had happened to old Herr Klein, their teacher, after he had told them the truth about East Germany selling weapons to other countries. But that had all changed. People were not afraid, now, to tell the truth. They were beaten up and imprisoned and still they told the truth. Hannah could hardly believe what she was hearing.

A red-haired woman stood up on the altar and talked about what had happened to her on the 6th October. 'I only got shoved and pushed around,' she said, 'but my friends got kicked and beaten and spent twenty-four hours locked up in a garage, forced to stand against a wall all the time.'

An old man stood up, on the balcony, and made his way to the microphone. He had a grey coat draped over his shoulders and it fell back as he reached out for the microphone. 'They broke my arm after the peace demonstration,' he said. 'They threw me down on the floor and I landed the wrong way up. But my broken arm is not the worst thing they've ever done to me.' A woman behind him pulled his coat over his shoulders again and put her arm round him as he leaned closer to the microphone. 'The worst thing they've done to me, to all of us, is that they've forced us to lie. I'm old and I've always known the whole thing was a lie. But some of you have grown up with this government. You've grown up so used to lying, that you don't even notice any more when you're lying and when you're telling the truth.'

The man wasn't looking at Hannah. There was no way he could have seen her, way down in the darkness of the huge church, lit only by a glow from hundreds of candles. But Hannah felt he was looking only at her, was talking only to her. She put up her hand and asked to speak. Then she stepped forward to the microphone in front of the altar.

'I was afraid to tell anyone before,' she said. Thousands of candles warmed the church with their light and Hannah wasn't afraid. She was only faintly aware that thousands of people were listening to her inside and outside the church. She felt at home there, standing on the altar. She felt she belonged.

'My mother wanted to leave the DDR,' she said. 'My father didn't want to leave. They used to argue so much about it, I thought they would have to divorce. But they still loved each other and they still loved me. Then one day they told me to tell my friends and the teachers at school that my parents had separated. They didn't tell me why I had to say that, but I was used to telling lies, so I did as they asked. Everyone believed me.'

She looked to the right and saw Steffi. In the light of her

139

candle Steffi's bruises had disappeared. Her black curls had firefly wisps of light dancing all around them.

'Now I know why my mother asked me to lie,' Hannah went on. 'She was planning to try to escape, and she knew that I would be taken away from my father and that he would be put in prison if we knew anything about her plan. So we had to go on lying.' Hannah took a deep breath and sighed. Thousands of candle flames flickered and swam on the sea of faces. 'Even after they shot my mother and killed her,' Hannah said, 'we had to go on telling lies. We had to pretend we hardly noticed she was gone. And when they shot her, we had to pretend we didn't care.'

Nobody moved. Hannah could feel that Steffi was looking at her, but she didn't turn round. Hannah closed her eyes and then opened them to see the bright pools of golden candle light. 'I just wanted to tell everyone that we did care.'

She stepped back and Steffi put her arms around her.

15

Hannah lay on the floor with her maths book in front of her. She hated maths. She didn't believe anyone would notice if she didn't do her homework. They had yet another new teacher now, because their maths teacher had gone to the West. Herr Pohl wasn't old and tired, like the other new teachers who had been arriving at their school: he was young and lazy. He had been trained to teach Russian, but no one needed Russian teachers, and he had to go wherever they sent him. He didn't like children.

Herr Pohl had no idea how to do the sort of maths they were doing and he tried to hide what he didn't know by shouting at them. At the beginning of every lesson, he walked into the room and said they were the laziest looking lot he had ever set eyes on. Then he told them to work in silence until they had completed ten pages of problems. But he never looked at what they had done. He read his newspaper during the lesson and got so annoyed when anyone asked him for help that everyone kept away from him. For homework he told them to do as many problems as they could manage in thirty-five minutes. He never looked at their homework either. Steffi said he wouldn't be able to tell them the right answers because he didn't have the Teachers' Answer Book. She said that their old teacher must have taken the answer book with him when he left for the West.

Hannah was almost asleep. She was sure her teacher wouldn't notice whether she had done her homework or not. But her father might ask her at breakfast and she would have to show it to him. Hannah's head dropped forward on to her arms and her eyes closed. It was half-past seven.

Even her father hadn't asked about her homework for the

last couple of days. For the last three months he had been as busy as he usually only was before a first night, staying very late at the theatre and leaving the flat almost as soon as Hannah got home from school. Hannah tried to open her eyes but they refused to move. She sighed. It felt so comfortable on the rug, with her head resting on her maths book. Perhaps her father would forget once again to ask about the homework.

When Hannah opened her eyes, it was nearly eight o'clock and the flat felt cold. She put a dressing-gown on over her clothes and went into the kitchen to make herself some cocoa. She was so tired. So much had happened in the last few weeks and still it felt as if nothing had happened. Nothing had really changed, except that Erich Honecker had gone and there was a new General Secretary with huge teeth and a sinister grin as wide as his face. Nothing would ever change. Hannah decided to watch the news and then go to bed. She had never felt so tired.

It was only after she had switched the television on and sat down on the sofa, that Hannah realized she had switched on the East German news. She wanted to watch West German television, but she was too tired to get up and change channels. She pulled a face as the Sandman programme finished and the little elf flew away in his balloon, sprinkling sparkling sand out on to the children down below and telling all the children to go to bed. She remembered how, when she was small, her mother had always read her a story after the Sandman programme, while her father watched the news.

The newsreader was the blonde woman Steffi hated. Hannah wished Steffi was with her. She told everyone she didn't mind being on her own when her father was out at work. She told them all she had got used to being on her own. But she liked it better when Steffi was there.

Hannah sat up straight. She had been thinking of Steffi and only half listening to the newsreader, but two sentences made their way through her tiredness, like blasts of cold wind waking her up.

'This evening, it has been announced that, as from midnight tonight, the people of East Germany will be able to travel freely between East and West Germany. It will no longer be necessary to obtain a visa before travelling.' The newsreader's face showed no emotion. She might as well have been reading the same news as every night, the news that yet another factory had successfully completed their five-year plan within four years and had been visited by Erich Honecker or Egon Krenz or one of the other top men in the party. The newsreader hadn't changed.

Hannah couldn't quite grasp what the words meant. 'The people of the DDR will be able to travel freely between East and West Germany.' She said the words again to herself. The rest of the news limped across the screen but Hannah saw only a blurred black and white image in slow motion. The newsreader was speaking German, but Hannah didn't understand her. People had talked about the freedom to travel to the West so many times at peace marches. But when the newsreader announced, on the official East German news, that everyone was free to travel, Hannah felt as if someone were speaking a foreign language, a language she didn't understand. How could one of the regular newsreaders on the official East German news say something like that?

She had said the people would not need a visa from midnight that night. Did that mean that people could just walk through the border checkpoints? Did that mean that people would be walking through and cycling through and driving through the Berlin Wall at the place where they had shot her mother? The idea was impossible. Hannah felt as if she had woken up from a dream and as if the words she had just heard were part of the dream. She got up slowly and changed over to West German television. Her legs and arms felt weak, as if she was recovering from a long illness.

She recognized the voice of one of the usual West German newsreaders, but the pictures on the screen looked very old. The newsreader said they were pictures of the Berlin Wall being built. People in old-fashioned clothes on the Eastern side of the Wall were throwing stones and bricks at the soldiers and prisoners at gunpoint who were building the Wall. The people on the Western side of the Wall were shaking their fists and throwing stones at the American tanks, whose soldiers seemed to be there to make sure they didn't fight to stop the Wall that cut their city in two. The soldiers in the East and the soldiers in the West were the only people who seemed to want the building to go on. The film clip finished and the newsreader continued, 'The last person to be shot before automatic guns were dismounted from the Wall was a young man who collapsed and died on the Western side barely seven months ago.' Hannah hadn't counted the months since they shot her mother. She had stopped counting. She realized her mother had been dead for nearly eight months.

The news was drawing to a close. 'Now here are the news headlines once again. It has been announced that as from midnight tonight, the people of the DDR will be free to travel between East and West Germany without visas.' Hannah switched the television off. The whole house was silent. What did the words mean? Hannah sat and heard the words in her head over and over again and still they refused to surrender their meaning.

She went out into the corridor, still with her dressing-gown on over her jeans and sweater. She knocked at Frau Goetz's door and heard someone fiddling with the chain. Then the old lady opened the door a crack, letting the milky pale light from her hall flow into the dark stairwell. 'Hannah, what's the matter? Nothing's happened, has it?' She started to remove the chain and stood aside to let Hannah into her flat.

'Did you watch the news?' Hannah went straight into Frau Goetz's living-room and curled up on her sofa.

'I don't believe a word of it, do you?' said Frau Goetz. 'I shan't be queuing up at midnight to go through the border, I can tell you. Who knows whether they'll let people back in again, once they've gone over to the West? I reckon they want people to leave so's they can get their hands on our furniture and anything else we can't take with us. The government's that hard up.'

She opened the tin she had always kept stocked with chocolate for Hannah, ever since they had moved into the flat next door when Hannah was three. Hannah took three cats' tongue chocolates. Frau Goetz pressed the lid back on to the tin. 'I once thought of going to the West,' she said. 'You can do it all legal when you get to pension age. But they told me I couldn't take my husband's stamp collection with me.' She opened the tin again and took two cats' tongues for herself. 'That did it,' she said. 'They won't catch me queuing up at the border at midnight, just so's they can get their hands on my stamps while I'm away.'

Hannah smiled. She couldn't believe that that was what the words meant, that people would be standing at the border at midnight that very night. Nothing happened so quickly in the DDR. She ran her tongue over her lips to taste the chocolate again and smiled because she couldn't remember the exact words the newsreader had said. She must have got it wrong. What the woman probably said was that the new leader of the DDR thought they might be able to travel without a visa at some time in the future, when the time was right. That was more like it. That was the sort of thing they were always saying.

It was warm in the old lady's flat. At nine o'clock, Frau Goetz said, 'When will your papa be home?'

'I don't know. He has a lot of work at the moment. I usually go to bed before he gets home.'

'You must get lonely, though.'

'Not really.'

Hannah didn't want to go back to her flat. She didn't want to be alone, thinking about her mother or the Wall. And she knew that if she went back into her own living-room she would put the television on again and try to hear more of the news she didn't believe. Frau Goetz's living room was quiet and warm.

'Ah well, you know you can always come to me, if you need

me.' Frau Goetz went into her bathroom and started to get ready for bed. The old lady always went to bed at nine, because all her working life she had got up at five. But Hannah didn't want to be alone in their flat. For eight months, she had stopped herself thinking too much about what the Wall had done to her mother. She didn't want to be alone with her thoughts when the unthinkable happened and the Wall lost its power.

The Wall looked harmless, like any other concrete wall, harmless and ugly. It wasn't like the brick wall near the church, a mosaic of different shades of red-brick, with Virginia creeper like a red and purple sunset in the autumn, then bare in the winter and then green through half the year. The Wall wasn't alive like the stone wall round their school playground, where yellow and purple flowers stuck out of the cracks at right angles and lichen turned the cracks into a trellis of green when it was damp. The Wall was cold and dirty, white and dead, but it looked harmless. That was what had made it so dangerous.

The Wall was like death, even for the living who dared to go beyond it. When people escaped through the Wall, it was as if they were dead. People talked about them as they do at a funeral. When one of their relatives escaped through the Wall, they would say, 'It was for the best,' and, 'It was what she would have wanted.' And friends who tried to comfort them said, 'You'll see them again—some day.' But everyone knew that when someone escaped through the Wall, it took years and years to see them again. Hannah knew that even if her mother had managed to escape they would still have had to behave as if she were dead. And they might never have seen her again. For the whole of Hannah's life, the Wall had been a monster with huge jaws, devouring anyone who dared to go near it.

The doorbell rang. Once, twice, three times, four times.

'Who on earth can that be, at this time of night? Don't you worry, Hannah. You can stay with me as long as you need to. Till your father gets home, if you want.' Frau Goetz shuffled towards the door and put the chain on.

'You don't need the chain,' Hannah said. 'My friend Steffi always rings at least four times.'

'Not at my door, she doesn't. It's very bad manners to ring four times like that, as if the person inside is deaf or something. Once is enough. Who's there?' Frau Goetz opened the door a crack and then banged it shut again. 'It is your friend,' she said. 'What's a young girl like that doing out at a time like this? Is she all right? Shall I let her in? What sort of parents has she got, letting her out at a time like this? Do you think she's run away from home?'

Steffi rang the doorbell again. Once, twice, three times. Frau Goetz managed to get the chain off just as she was about to ring for the fourth time.

Steffi put her arms round Frau Goetz and gave her a hug. 'Isn't it wonderful?' Frau Goetz pulled her dressing-gown tightly around herself and her mouth dropped open and stayed open as Steffi strode into the flat. Steffi grabbed hold of Hannah and hugged her, too. 'I knew you'd be here. We tried and tried to phone you at home, but there was no answer. My mum's waiting downstairs, so we can all go together.' She put her arms round Frau Goetz again. 'We've got room for you, too,' she said. 'You can't go to bed on a night like this.'

'Oh, yes I can.' Frau Goetz picked up the magazine she had been reading before Hannah arrived. 'If it's true what they say, the Wall will still be open tomorrow. And when's the last time you remember that lot telling the truth? If it's not true, there'll be plenty of people'll wish they'd stayed at home, like I'm going to do.'

Steffi grinned. 'But if it is true, what they say, there'll be millions of people wishing they could have been there at the Wall, like we're going to be. Come on, Hannah. Get your coat.'

Hannah kissed Frau Goetz. 'We'll go past the theatre on the way to the Wall,' she said, 'so Papa will know where I am.'

Hannah had often been to the theatre with her mother. And she knew which door she had to go through to find her father when the performance was over. 'They'll have finished by now,' she said. Steffi's mother sat and waited in the car while the two girls went round to the door near the actor's entrance. But the door was locked and they had to go round to the front of the theatre and into the main lobby. The huge, red-carpeted room was deserted, and loud voices came from within the theatre.

Steffi tried to push open one of the doors, but at first it wouldn't budge. 'I think it's locked,' she said. 'Why have they locked all the doors? What if there's a fire?'

She pushed again and this time the door gave way and Steffi almost fell on top of a crowd of people who were sitting in the gangway. The theatre was packed. People were sitting two to a seat and on every available step in the gangway. Some were even sitting with their legs dangling over the balconies. But the play was over. The curtains were closed and the spotlights were trained on a woman who was speaking.

'What's happening?' Steffi managed to squeeze in and sit down next to a woman on the floor.

'It's the discussion after the play,' the woman said. 'They have them every night now. They just can't keep people out.'

'But they don't let all these people come to watch the play, do they?'

The woman shook her head. 'After it's over. They want to talk. Everyone wants to talk about what we can do to change things. And what they're up to with these new changes in travel laws.'

Steffi was impatient. The people in the theatre had obviously only heard half the news. They wouldn't be sitting there talking if they knew what had happened, if they knew that the world had changed. They'd all be heading for the Wall. Steffi stood up to tell them, but Hannah grabbed hold of her arm.

'Look, my papa's going to talk. Why is he up on stage? He's not one of the actors.'

The woman turned round and looked at Hannah. 'Is that your father?' Other people all around them turned and looked at her, too. The woman whispered. 'He's wonderful. But you must know all that already. I met him at the demo last week.' She took hold of Hannah's hand. 'Look after him, won't you.'

'See! I told you I saw him at that demonstration,' said Steffi.

'Shush!' Hannah wanted to listen.

Her father said he wasn't going to give a long speech. He reminded them of the peace demonstrations in the churches on Monday. 'We must keep telling the government what we want,' he said. 'Free and fair elections. Freedom for everybody to travel between East and West.' Then he asked for questions from the audience. Hannah put her hand up, but there were at least ten questions from other people. They were all asking whether the rumours were true, about people being free to travel, and nobody knew. It looked as if they'd been so busy at the theatre that none of them had watched the news that night. And they had all learned not to trust rumours.

Then the floodlight picked Hannah out and she stepped towards the nearest microphone. 'I think the next question is from over near the door.' Hannah's father pointed towards her and then shaded his eyes to try and see who was going to speak. 'What's your question, please?'

The floodlight trained on Hannah's father and the other light on her made the rest of the theatre dark so that it was as if she was alone in the room with him. She was annoyed. 'My question is: why is it all right for you to go on peace demonstrations when you won't let me go?' The audience laughed and people started to clap.

'Hannah . . .'

'Papa. You said it was dangerous for me to go because I might get put in prison. What would I have done if they'd put you in prison?'

Again, people laughed and clapped, but Hannah's father put his hand up and they fell silent. 'I had to do this, Hannah.

149

You know that. I had to do this work. And I didn't want to worry you.'

'Same with me. And Opa and Oma. We told you we had to march that night in Leipzig, but you still got mad at us.'

People laughed and clapped even louder than before and Steffi stood up next to Hannah, trying to wrestle the microphone from her hand. Their loud whispers could be heard right up on the stage and as far away as the seats up on the third gallery of the building. 'Are you going to tell them, or shall I?' The audience heard scratches and squeaks.

'Steffi, I'm speaking. I've got the microphone.'

'Well, get on with it then. Tell them what's happened.'

Hannah's father smiled. 'I gather there's something you want to tell us.'

'That's what we came here for,' Hannah shouted. 'Papa, everyone keeps asking you whether it's true about us being able to travel. Well, it's been on West TV as well as on ours. Somebody in here must have seen it! They've opened the Wall.'

Hannah's father tried to say something, but his words were lost in the sound of cheering. People were hugging and kissing complete strangers. Hannah and Steffi slowly made their way to the stage with people wanting to shake their hands from every side while the huge crowd pushed towards the door, everyone making for the Wall.

It took more than half an hour before the crowd had left the theatre and Hannah and Steffi with Hannah's father, finally made their way back to the car. A woman had given Steffi's mother three red roses as she left the theatre and she gave one each to Steffi and Hannah. Hannah's father said they wouldn't find another place to park that night, so they left the car, linked arms and walked the rest of the way to the Wall.

They were used to queuing, but Hannah had never been in a queue which moved so quickly. 'They're not even checking identity cards,' someone shouted from way up ahead of them. The sky was bright with the floodlights which were always trained on no-man's land next to the Wall. From over the other side, at the point where Hannah knew the border crossing must be, she saw hundreds of flashing lights, like a never-ending firework display.

'There's crowds waiting over the other side. Can't you hear them?'

'They've got TV cameras, too.'

'What for?'

Everyone was shouting and laughing and jumping up and down. It was as if the curtains had opened on a new play, with the brightly lit-up Wall as backdrop to whatever was going to happen next.

'We're only going over to have a quick look.' Two old ladies in identical beige overcoats were just behind Hannah in the queue.

'Oh, yes.' The second one had a green woolly hat and black-rimmed spectacles. 'We're only going to see what it's like in the West. Then we're coming back home. It's way past our bed-time.'

The boy in front of Hannah shouted back at them, 'You'll have to stay a bit if you want to get your money.'

'What money?'

'I've heard that anyone who visits West Berlin gets 100 marks—West money. You can buy good things with West money.'

'Ooh, well, we'll have to stay then.' The old lady pulled her woolly hat over her ears and stamped her feet in their zip-fronted boots.

'There's a soldier, Papa.' Hannah leaned against her father's grey woollen coat, where it was nice and warm out of the wind. Then she grabbed hold of his lapels. 'He might have been the one who shot her, Papa. It could have been any one of them.' She started to cry and buried her face in his coat, not wanting to look at the soldiers marching up and down, laughing and joking and keeping people in line.

151

Hannah's father stroked her hair. Steffi put her arm round Hannah's shoulders. Hannah looked up and saw that her father was crying, too. It was the first time she had seen him crying. They were free to go through the Wall. That was what her mother had wanted. They were free to go through the Wall and then come back to their home in the East. That was what her father had been fighting for. And Hannah was free to speak the truth, the truth about how she had felt when her mother died.

'Oh, look. Oh, look. We're nearly there. That soldier's letting them through really quickly. Make sure we get in his queue. What are all those lights, flashing on and off? They're too low down for fireworks.'

'They're cameras flashing, people taking photographs.'

A policeman came and asked the two old ladies to get back into the line.

'We're not staying long,' they said.

Steffi grinned. 'We can always come back again tomorrow if it's as good as people say.'

'We're going to a restaurant with Steffi's father,' her mother added. 'He phoned us up when he heard the news. They've got restaurants open almost all night in West Berlin.'

'Make sure you come back, Hannah.' Steffi looked suddenly worried, as if they were all about to set out on a trip round the world, a trip from which they might never return.

'Don't be stupid. I only want to take a look. I don't want to be a Westi. I'll be coming back with Papa.'

They were almost at the crossing. Hannah had shuffled along with her face still hidden in her father's coat, not wanting to look at the soldiers with their machine-guns. The soldier at the checkpoint asked the boy in front of Hannah where his parents were and made him show his pass. One of the old ladies whispered, 'That gun looks fierce,' and shouted out to him. 'You're not going to shoot us with that thing, are you, sonny?'

The soldier turned round and smiled. 'I've never used it. Except a bit in training. Today's my first day.' He was holding